FROM THE
NANCY DREW FILES

THE CASE: Nancy takes center stage in a show of magic, mystery, and menace.

CONTACT: Magician Adriana Polidori thought she knew every trick in the book—until crime got into the act.

SUSPECTS: Mikhail Grigov—A master knife-thrower, he now has but one aim in life: targeting former girlfriend Adriana Polidori.

Freda Clarke—Her son was injured in an amusement park accident, and she's determined to make someone pay.

Benny Gotnick—A longtime employee at Riverfront who was suddenly fired, he might easily come back . . . with some heat of his own.

COMPLICATIONS: Nancy's learning more and more about the shadowy schemes behind the scenes at Riverfront. But the more dirt she digs up, the more dangerous life becomes . . . for Ned!

Books in The Nancy Drew Files® Series

The Nancy Drew Files™

Case 94

Illusions of Evil
Carolyn Keene

AN ARCHWAY PAPERBACK
Published by POCKET BOOKS
New York   London   Toronto   Sydney   Tokyo   Singapore

AN ARCHWAY PAPERBACK *Original*

An Archway Paperback published by
POCKET BOOKS, a division of Simon & Schuster Inc.
1230 Avenue of the Americas, New York, NY 10020

Copyright © 1994 Simon & Schuster Inc.
Produced by Mega-Books of New York, Inc.

ISBN: 0-671-79486-8

First Archway Paperback printing April 1994

10 9 8 7 6 5 4 3 2 1

NANCY DREW, AN ARCHWAY PAPERBACK and colophon
are registered trademarks of Simon & Schuster Inc.

THE NANCY DREW FILES is a trademark
of Simon & Schuster Inc.

Cover art by Cliff Miller

Printed in the U.S.A.

IL 6+

Chapter

One

"THIS IS GOING to be awesome!" Ned Nickerson exclaimed. "I get to spend my ten days of spring break with my girl, and the very first night she gets free tickets to Riverfront Park!"

Ned leaned across from the passenger seat of Nancy's blue Mustang and wrapped Nancy in a hug. "Boy, did I miss you!"

"Same here, Nickerson," Nancy said, resting her head briefly on his shoulder.

"It's been too long," Ned murmured into Nancy's ear.

George Fayne coughed pointedly from the back, where she sat sideways, her long legs stretched out across both seats. "Save the lovey-dovey stuff for later, okay? We have to get to Adriana's show."

"Right," said Nancy, sitting up and starting the car.

"I can't believe Adriana Polidori is one of your father's clients," Ned said as Nancy pulled the Mustang away from the curb. "She's one of the most famous magicians in the world."

Nancy, Ned, and their good friend George were headed for Riverfront Park, an amusement park just south of Conklin Falls, about twenty miles from River Heights, where George and Nancy lived. The free passes had arrived at Carson Drew's law office, compliments of Adriana Polidori herself.

"I'm still surprised that Adriana decided to take over the park after her uncle Nicos died last fall," Nancy commented. "Dad says she plans to give up touring and settle down here for good."

"It *does* seem like an odd career move," Ned agreed.

"I don't know about that," George said. "Remember when we went to that rock concert at the park last summer? The auditorium is huge—it would be perfect for a magic show. Besides, what magician wouldn't want her own stage, where she could permanently rig up equipment for really spectacular illusions?"

Nancy drove out of town and got on the parkway headed north toward Conklin Falls. During the ride, she and George caught Ned up on what had been going on in River Heights,

2

including how Nancy had gotten involved in a big murder case while serving as a volunteer at the city's teen center hotline. Ned was a student at Emerson College, a two-hour drive from River Heights, so he and Nancy didn't get to spend much time together during the school year.

Nancy stole a glance at Ned. It was such a treat having him there! She couldn't help sighing.

Ned caught her gazing at him and chastised her gently. "Keep your eyes on the road, Drew."

Nancy grinned and rubbed Ned's arm playfully. "Don't kid yourself. You're not that distracting, Nickerson."

"Hey, look," George broke in, pointing up ahead. "Talk about spectacular!"

From the parkway exit ramp, they could see the lights of the amusement park glittering against the clear early-evening sky. As Nancy turned onto the road that led toward the Muskoka River, she spotted the roller coaster, Ferris wheel, and parachute jump.

"I can't wait!" George cried. "I'm going on the roller coaster. And I'm going to eat cotton candy until I'm stuffed. Who's up for it?"

"Me!" Ned said.

"But not until after the magic show," Nancy added.

"Well, sure," said George. "We can't miss Adriana's act."

Soon they were driving through the gates of

Riverfront Park. The parking lot was jammed. Even on a chilly Tuesday evening in April, Adriana was attracting a sizable crowd.

"Isn't it a bit early in the season to open an amusement park?" George asked.

"Actually, the grand opening isn't until the beginning of May," Nancy explained. "These first few weeks are sort of a dress rehearsal. My dad said Adriana wants to try out her new act on an audience to work out the bugs. She also decided to open a number of the rides and attractions, but she won't have everything up and running until May."

Nancy found a parking place at the far end of the lot. The three of them got out, then Nancy locked the car, and they headed for the entrance. They showed their passes to the man at the booth, then joined the crowd along the midway. It was a beautiful evening but definitely chilly. Nancy was glad she'd worn her leather bomber jacket, jeans, and a sweater. Ned wrapped an arm around her shoulder, and Nancy smiled up at him.

"Don't you love this old place?" she asked.

The midway was a broad, gravel-covered walkway that ran from the entrance to a plaza perched high on the cliffs above the river. It twinkled with festive lights and was lined with dozens of game and refreshment booths. Barkers called to Nancy and her friends from the booths, challenging them to win prizes by tossing rings or shooting duck decoys or ringing a bell with a whack of a sledgehammer.

The brightly lit rides surrounding the midway whirled against the dark sky. Nancy noticed a line at the Ferris wheel and could hear joyful, giddy screams from the cars suspended high above her. Raucous music filled the air, making her head spin.

"You bet I love it," Ned said. "I remember coming here when I was a kid. I'm glad Adriana is going to keep it open."

"I just wish Bess were with us," George lamented, running a hand through her short brown hair. Bess Marvin was George's cousin and the girls' best friend.

"Maybe she'll go to a theme park while she's in Florida with her family," Nancy said.

"Maybe. But only Riverfront has the Typhoon," George declared. She gazed longingly at the big roller coaster as they walked by. Its towering latticework of steel beams supported tracks that twisted and dipped like the rings of intertwined pretzels. As two trains of four cars each plummeted down the steep hills, the riders on the Typhoon shrieked and raised their arms straight over their heads.

Nancy could sense Ned and George's excitement as they watched the cars sail by. She checked her watch and said, "Ten minutes until Adriana's show. You guys will just have to wait to ride the Typhoon."

5

George seemed to be dejected for a moment, but then her expression brightened. "All right! Let's get going or we might miss her act."

They found a sign for the auditorium and hurried in that direction. The crowd thickened as they neared the huge brick and glass building. Above the entrance was a marquee. Appearing Tonight: Adriana Polidori, the World's Greatest Illusionist, its bright lights announced.

Ushers guided Nancy and her friends into the auditorium and to their seats in the second row. Heavy blue velvet curtains hid the stage, and the audience around them buzzed, anticipating the show.

Soon the lights dimmed, and out of the darkness the beam of a single spotlight hit the curtains. Then a violin played a haunting gypsy melody. The curtains parted just enough to allow a solitary figure to pass through. Adriana Polidori stepped into the spotlight, to the wild applause of the audience.

Ned leaned over to Nancy. "I guess everyone's as excited as we are to see Adriana in person," he whispered.

Nancy studied Adriana as she held up her hand to silence the crowd. She was in her midthirties, a tall, strikingly beautiful woman with dramatic features and thick jet black hair. She wore an elegant floor-length black gown with a halter neck and long black gloves.

"I guess we can be pretty sure that she doesn't have anything up her sleeves," George joked.

Now the audience hushed, and Adriana leaned toward them, a mischievous gleam in her startling green eyes. She gestured sinuously with her hands and arms, drawing them in.

"Good evening, ladies and gentlemen," she said, her voice a whisper picked up by a microphone Nancy knew was hidden on her costume. "Welcome to my new home. Riverfront Park was my home once before, when I was a little girl, and it was here, in a place of marvels and joy, that I learned about magic. I want to share the dreams of that little girl with you tonight."

Adriana gestured dramatically toward the curtains. As they parted, a smoky, multicolored haze poured from the opening. More lights came up on stage, and the audience murmured appreciatively at the scene revealed. The set depicted a fanciful Arabian garden surrounded by domes and minarets. Colored fog a foot deep swirled around the floor of the stage. Above, a bright crescent moon shone in a sky filled with jewellike stars. Nancy was dazzled.

As the violin played, Adriana began to dance. For a second she vanished behind a palm tree, and when she appeared again, she wore scarlet harem pants, a brocaded vest, and many swirling veils. The audience applauded at her remarkable transformation.

7

Over the music came the sound of Adriana's voice, rich, full, hypnotic, no longer a whisper. "The girl dreamed that she was a princess, imprisoned in the garden of an evil wizard. She danced to soothe her loneliness. Her only companions were the creatures of her imagination."

As she danced, she released several veils, one by one. Each of them swirled as it fell, then rose again, as if by itself. Soon there were four of these silk shadows dancing with her.

"Are they real dancers or what?" Ned asked Nancy.

"They couldn't be," Nancy whispered back, mesmerized. "But they sure look real. I wonder how she does it."

"You guys," George scolded them. "Don't try to figure it out. You'll ruin it!"

The music built to a crescendo, then suddenly stopped. Adriana froze in place. The dancing veils stopped, too, trembling a bit as Adriana frowned at them.

"But these companions only reminded the princess that she was alone," she told the audience, then clapped her hands imperiously. As if following her command, the veils dropped to the floor. The audience applauded, enchanted by her showmanship.

The music began again as Adriana said, "The princess knew she must escape the garden and venture out into the great world beyond. But how?" Adriana swirled around, and when she faced the audience again, she had a shiny brass lamp in one hand. Her face shone with joy and wonder.

Nancy watched as Adriana rubbed the lantern and purple smoke began to pour from it, rising toward the ceiling in a dense column. Gradually the smoke took the shape of a huge genie looming over the magician. Adriana drew back in fear but then leaned forward as though listening as the genie spoke to her.

"The genie promised the princess only one wish, but she knew at once what it must be. Something to take her away!" The genie bowed once to Adriana, then broke apart as though scattered by a breeze.

The audience sat spellbound. Adriana turned her attention to the fog billowing around her feet. She began to wave her arms in front of her, and a Persian carpet rose out of the haze. Soon it floated four feet off the floor, undulating in response to Adriana's gestures.

Nancy scanned the stage to see if she could figure out how the carpet was operated. She quickly gave up and let Adriana's magic work, her gaze riveted on the patterned rug as it dipped low for Adriana to leap onto it. It swooped high into the air, Adriana riding it like Aladdin! The audience gasped in amazement.

"But the evil wizard would not let her escape so easily," Adriana went on. A dark figure in a black turban and robe appeared atop one of the minarets. He snapped his fingers, and a ring of fire formed in front of Adriana. The carpet hesitated in midair, then flew right through the fiery hoop. Adriana escaped!

Still up in the air on the flying carpet, she laughed at the evil wizard, who stood shaking his fist at her. The audience laughed.

"See?" Nancy whispered to Ned. "The way she went through the ring proves that there are no strings holding the carpet up!"

Just then Nancy spotted several small tongues of flame licking at the back corner of the flying carpet.

"Ned, George," Nancy said, her fear sounding an alarm. "Look!"

"The carpet's on fire," George said, rising out of her seat. "That's not supposed to happen, is it?"

Nancy clutched the arms of her chair.

Someone at the back of the audience screamed.

Startled, Adriana turned and saw the orange glow that had now engulfed the carpet's tassled fringe. Nancy could tell by the magician's expression that something terrible was happening.

Adriana took a step toward the fire, raising her foot to stamp it out. Before she could move, though, the carpet erupted in flames!

Chapter
Two

ADRIANA! NO!"

The shout came from a tall man in a dark suit who'd sprung up from his seat in the front row. With surprising agility, he leapt onto the stage, tore off his jacket, and started beating the flames with his jacket.

The rest of the audience rose almost as one when it became clear that Adriana's act had gone terribly wrong.

"Come on, she needs help!" Nancy cried to Ned and George.

She raced for the steps at the side of the stage. Ned and George followed, carrying their jackets. The man was still beating at the flames, which had spread to Adriana's costume. The magician still hadn't jumped down—perhaps she was in shock. Ned and George joined the man, while crew members ran out from the wings.

Nancy dashed offstage and spotted what was needed—a fire extinguisher. She grabbed it and vaulted toward Adriana.

"Stand back!" Nancy called out. Then she shot several hard blasts of foam at Adriana and the flaming carpet. The magician reeled, but the extinguisher did its job.

"Adriana," the tall man cried, pulling her down from the carpet and into his arms.

George and Ned appeared at Nancy's side. "Who's that guy?" George asked.

"I haven't the vaguest idea," Nancy replied.

As the stage manager reassured the audience that Adriana was all right, the curtain came down behind him. Nancy doused the flying carpet with a few more shots of foam, putting the fire out completely.

"What do you think happened, Nan?" Ned asked, whispering.

"I'm not sure, but you can bet I'm going to find out," Nancy said. "First let's make sure Adriana's all right."

"I think her friend is doing a pretty good job of that," George said with a slight smile.

Clutching Adriana to him, the man rose to his full height. He had a shock of dark hair and a small gold hoop dangled from his left ear. At his side, Adriana looked shaken. The man stroked her hair gently and led her offstage.

Meanwhile, the house lights came on and ushers began guiding people out of the auditorium.

Nancy, George, and Ned quickly caught up with Adriana backstage. "Excuse me," Nancy said, calling after the magician. "My friends and I wanted to make sure you're okay."

Adriana turned. She was deathly pale, but a look of gratitude passed over her face. She gripped Nancy's forearm with a very strong hand. "I'm fine. You saved my life, young lady. How can I thank you?"

The dark-haired man stood behind Adriana, silent and frowning.

"You can let me take a look at your flying carpet," Nancy replied. "I'd like to find out how the fire started."

"She's a detective," George explained.

The magician frowned.

Nancy laughed lightly. "My name is Nancy Drew," she said.

"Carson's daughter!" the woman exclaimed. "You even look a little like him around the eyes." She clasped Nancy's hand in both of hers. "Your father is a wonderful lawyer. He handled my uncle Nicos's estate. And when I came here several months ago, he became my first friend."

"You sent him tickets for tonight, remember?" Nancy said. "He was tied up, so he gave them to us." Nancy gestured to her companions. "These

13

are my friends, George Fayne and Ned Nickerson."

Adriana shook their hands, then turned back to Nancy. "Your father has told me about you. He's very proud of your detective work."

"And she's just as good as he said," Ned added.

Adriana dropped her head. "I could use a detective," she said softly.

"You don't think the fire was an accident, do you?" Nancy asked.

Adriana ran her fingers through her tousled hair, then looked up. "We are very careful here. My crew has been with me for years, through all my touring. This kind of thing has never happened before."

"Do you have any idea how the fire started?" Nancy pressed.

"The ring trick has been in my act before. My stage manager, André, douses the carpet and my costume with flame retardant," she explained.

"I see," Nancy said.

Adriana straightened. "I'll have André show you how it works. If you can find out how this happened . . ."

"Of course," Nancy assured her. "I'll do whatever I can to help."

Relief softened Adriana's face. "André!" she called out.

The man who had made the announcement to the audience came forward. He was a short man in his twenties with curly blond hair. "Please show Ms. Drew how the carpet trick works," Adriana said, her voice suddenly clipped and professional.

Then the magician turned to Nancy, Ned, and George. "I'll be in my dressing room. Could you meet me there in half an hour?" she asked.

Nancy nodded.

"By then I should have recovered. And maybe you'll have some news for me," Adriana added.

"I hope so," Nancy said.

Then Adriana took the tall man's arm and swept away.

"Amazing!" Ned exclaimed, following Adriana with his eyes.

"Don't get any ideas, Nickerson," Nancy said. "Just because she's beautiful. And talented."

"Don't worry, Drew," he replied teasingly. "You've got your own kind of magic."

Behind Ned, George groaned. Then the three friends turned to Adriana's stage manager, who led them over to where the flying carpet still stood, half-burned, in the middle of the stage. Someone had already mopped up the foam from the fire extinguisher, but the smell of smoke and chemicals lingered.

"It looks like Adriana will have to make some serious repairs," said Ned as he surveyed the damage. A third of the carpet was completely burned, and the rest was badly singed. "How does this thing work anyway?"

André jogged offstage left, calling, "Just watch," as he went.

Suddenly Nancy heard a soft mechanical whir, and the carpet slowly lowered, then rose.

"Wow!" George said.

Then André rejoined them and explained, "The carpet's on a hydraulic lift built into the stage floor."

Stepping closer, Nancy saw that the carpet actually lay atop a column covered with mirrors. "I get it," she said. "The mirrors reflect the set, so the audience sees the minarets instead of the lift."

"Right," André said. "And there are rollers underneath the carpet to make it look like it's undulating. With all that smoke swirling around, no one can tell that it isn't the real thing." He stood back and brushed his hands against his worn blue jeans.

"But none of that explains the fire," said Ned.

"That's true," Nancy agreed, lightly touching the rug. Then she frowned and leaned over. She sniffed the blackened fabric. "Kerosene," she said.

Ned put his nose to the carpet, too. "You're right!" he exclaimed. His eyes widened. "Someone coated this carpet with kerosene."

André looked confounded. "No way," he said. "This baby gets sprayed with a flame retardant called No-Flame every night, not kerosene.

16

That's how Adriana makes it through the ring," he stated almost defiantly.

Nancy could see that the stage manager was upset. "Just tell me where you keep the retardant," Nancy said mildly.

André shrugged. "Backstage, in the rear on the right. There's a prop and pyrotechnics room."

"Thanks, André," Nancy said, leading the way back to the prop room. The door was open, and it didn't take Nancy long to find the metal tank labeled No-Flame. It had a nozzle and hose attached to it. Nancy unscrewed the hose and sniffed the tank.

"Kerosene," she confirmed for George and Ned, who stood beside her. "I'm going to report this to Adriana. Why don't you guys go on ahead? I know how much you want to ride the Typhoon. I'll catch up with you there."

"Are you sure you don't want us to come with you?" George asked.

"I'm positive," Nancy answered. "It's probably best if I break the news to Adriana by myself."

George and Ned took off toward the exit at the back of the auditorium, while Nancy went in search of Adriana's dressing room. The hall leading off the backstage area had several doors, and one of them was marked with a star and had Adriana's name on it. Just before she knocked, Nancy heard a man's voice raised in anger. As soon as she rapped on the door, the voice stopped.

"Come in" came Adriana's response.

Nancy stepped inside and was instantly awed by Adriana's dressing room. One entire wall was covered in mirrors, with a long makeup table facing it. The room was furnished with a plush sofa, an armchair, and a coffee table, and there was a small kitchenette in an alcove off to the side. A door on the left led to a bathroom, and another on the right opened into a huge walk-in closet filled with colorful costumes.

"This place is great," Nancy said, admiring it. "You could almost live here."

Adriana, who had put on a long terrycloth robe, laughed. "That's exactly what I did for the first month after I moved to Conklin Falls, but then I found a nice apartment in town." The magician paused, then gestured toward the man who'd come to her rescue at the scene of the accident. He was sitting on the sofa, paring his fingernails with a knife that had an intricately carved pearl handle.

Adriana noticed Nancy's surprised expression and laughed. "I want you to meet my old touring partner, Mikhail Grigov, otherwise known as Sabre the Blademaster."

"The Blademaster?" Nancy echoed.

Mikhail bowed his head and extended his hand to Nancy. Then he waved his knife in the air. "I am famous for my knife-throwing skills," he said. "Hence, the Blademaster."

"Misha has been performing in Chicago," Adriana explained. "But he had a week off before going on to Minneapolis so he came down to visit me."

"Adriana is telling only half the story," he said, giving the magician an intense look. "I came to beg her to give up this ridiculous idea. She's a performer, not an amusement park manager! She belongs with me on the road."

Adriana laughed and gazed at him affectionately. "Oh, Misha," she said, "you never give up." She moved gracefully toward her closet. "Please excuse me. I just finished washing up. Now I want to change into street clothes."

Nancy had hoped to tell the magician what she had learned, but Adriana disappeared into her closet.

Nancy realized she would have to wait until the woman returned. She turned to Misha. "Are you staying in Conklin Falls?" she asked.

He looked up, then placed his knife on the coffee table. "Yes. In a terrible motel with a very hard bed." He shook his head. "The things I do for that woman—"

"It's lucky you were here tonight," Nancy said. "You knew what was happening before anyone else did."

At that, his eyes flashed. "Of course. I have been working with Adriana for years."

They talked casually for a few minutes until Adriana reappeared in a crisp white blouse, faded jeans, and soft suede boots.

"So, Nancy, did you learn anything?" Adriana asked.

When Nancy explained how the flame retardant had been replaced with kerosene, Adriana's face went white, and Misha jumped up from where he was sitting. "You see!" he shouted. "This place is cursed. It's that Freda Clarke woman. She will do anything to shut you down. Adriana, please. Sell the park. Listen to me!"

Nancy watched as Adriana's eyes filled with tears. Finally the magician regained her composure and said, "Misha, I've heard all this before. Please go now. I want to speak with Nancy— alone."

Misha stood up, his mouth set in a determined line. "I will go. But I will not give up. This park is dangerous, Adriana."

With that, he left. As soon as the door closed behind him, the magician let out a long sigh. "Please sit," she told Nancy, and went to the kitchenette where she put a kettle on the stove. Then she spoke. "After my uncle Nicos died, I *was* tempted to sell Riverfront Park. But instead, I decided to take it over myself. I want to turn it into a truly modern theme park. I even have a name for it—Polidori's Magicworld." She laughed. "Uncle Nicos would have loved it."

"It sounds great," Nancy said.

"I grew up here, you know," Adriana went on, "with Nicos." A pained expression crossed her face. "But when he died so tragically . . ."

"What do you mean?" Nancy asked.

Adriana clasped her hands to her chest. "He was electrocuted while making a repair on the midway. Apparently, he neglected to turn off a circuit," she said tonelessly.

Nancy's eyes widened. "And this woman Misha mentioned?"

"Freda Clarke." Adriana thought for a moment, then said, "Her son was injured on the roller coaster last summer when Uncle Nicos was still running the park. The state inspectors ruled it an accident, but she's been trying to close Riverfront ever since, picketing and threatening lawsuits and such. That's why I consulted your father."

"Would she go so far as to sabotage your act?" Nancy asked.

"Misha thinks so," said Adriana. "I made the mistake of mentioning Freda to him, and now he thinks she's behind what happened tonight."

Nancy frowned. "That seems a little far-fetched. But we have to include her as a suspect. Maybe she had an accomplice inside the park—someone with access to the tank. Any ideas?"

Adriana shook her head, then turned at the sound of the whistling teakettle. She turned off the stove, then rubbed her temples and said, "I'm sorry, Nancy. I'm grateful for your help, but

21

suddenly I'm very tired. Perhaps we can continue this tomorrow?"

"Sure," Nancy replied, standing up. "You've had a terrible night. But don't worry. I'm going to get to the bottom of this."

"Thank you," Adriana said, gripping Nancy's hand.

"I'll see you tomorrow," Nancy said, and closed the door behind her.

Even though it was ten o'clock, the park was still crammed with visitors. Nancy strolled along the midway on her way to the roller coaster, her mind still on Adriana's problems. But as she approached the Typhoon, she snapped out of her reverie. She heard screams. People were rushing past her.

"What's happening?" she asked the man beside her.

She didn't wait for an answer. Looking up, she saw that one car in a train had derailed on a banked curve of the coaster. The cars behind it were still on the track. The two passengers in the lead car were in trouble, though. Their car had jumped the track and was dangling at least thirty feet above the ground.

There was a hollow feeling in the pit of her stomach as Nancy pushed her way through the crowd at the foot of the ride. When she was close enough to get a good look at the couple still seated in the front car, she gasped.

It was Ned and George!

Chapter
Three

N**ED!**" N**ANCY SCREAMED.** "George!"

They were suspended in the car nearly upside down. Only their safety straps and a bar kept them from plummeting to the ground.

People around Nancy were pointing and murmuring, their faces full of fear. She noticed that the second train of cars had avoided disaster and was stopped at a low place on the coaster. Its passengers were already scrambling down to safety. Then she saw a man halfway up the rise, where the first train had hit trouble. He was climbing the tracks. In minutes he reached the jeopardized train and bent over to the passengers in the last car.

Nancy heard sirens wail in the distance, but she wasn't about to sit still while her friends' lives

23

were at stake. She pushed her way through the crowd. In seconds she reached the steel lattice-work side of the coaster under the spot where the lead car had gone over the edge. As she grabbed onto a crossbeam and started to climb up, she heard someone call her name.

"Nancy! Wait!"

It was Adriana. The park owner was running toward her, her black hair flying out of its bar-rettes. When she arrived, Adriana was breathless. "You had just left when my stage manager told me there had been an accident. I raced over here." She looked up at the roller coaster and said, "I'm going with you."

Before Nancy could say a word, Adriana was climbing up beside her. The latticework beams provided footing and handholds. They were both out of breath when they reached the top and scrambled over the guardrail onto the tracks.

The wind whipped Nancy's hair into her eyes. She pushed it away, crossed the tracks to the side where George and Ned had gone over, then leaned over the rail so that she could see the car in peril. In it, George and Ned were like a pair of wide-eyed puppets, frozen in place, clutching the steel bar in front of them. Nancy tried to swallow her fear and get their attention. "Hey, Ned, George, don't worry—we'll get you down!"

Ned turned toward her. He was bleeding from a nasty gash in his forehead.

Just then Adriana nudged Nancy. She turned and saw that the man who'd climbed up the tracks was helping the passengers in the last three cars out of their safety harnesses. The burly man wore a gray worksuit with a Riverfront Park insignia above the breast pocket and a red bandanna around his neck.

"That's Rand Hagan, my chief engineer and ride supervisor," Adriana explained, breathless.

On the tracks behind Hagan, Nancy could see that other gray-suited park workers had followed Hagan up the tracks. Like a human chain, they were now guiding the frightened riders who'd been released down the steep slope.

Nancy and Adriana turned back to the first car, which was connected to the rest of the train by a solid metal hitch. Nancy noticed the heavy-duty hosing that lined the tracks firmly gripping the front wheels of the cars; she was relieved to see that the coaster's brake system had apparently worked. The roller coaster wasn't going anywhere. What about George and Ned, dangling precariously in the car that had gone over the edge?

Nancy thought fast, then lowered herself to the foot-wide metal easement bordering the tracks. Lying on the easement and gripping the guardrail with one hand, she reached down toward her friends. Her hand touched the car just behind George's head, but she could reach no farther.

"Hold on," came a gruff voice behind her.

Nancy pulled herself back and saw that Rand Hagan had come to her side.

"What are we going to do?" Adriana asked tensely as Nancy carefully stood up.

"If I lie down and lean over, I can reach them," Hagan replied. "But I'll need your help. You two have to hold my feet." He lowered himself so that his stomach was on the metal easement and the toes of his boots were wedged underneath the steel lip of the tracks. Nancy grabbed one of Hagan's legs with both her hands and held on. Adriana clutched Hagan's other leg and did the same.

"Okay, kids," he said, "I'm coming to get you. When I start unbuckling your harness, hang on to the bar. For a couple of seconds, until I can get a grip on you, that's all that'll be keeping you from falling. I'll pull you out just as soon as I can."

Nancy could only clutch onto Hagan and hope. The seconds passed like hours, and a thin film of sweat gathered on her forehead. Next to her, Adriana was ashen.

"Just hang on to that bar," she heard Hagan say again.

"Got it," came George's voice, weak but clear.

Several minutes later Nancy felt Hagan's body contract as he pulled George up and over the back of the car and onto the tracks. Even as her friend struggled over the edge and collapsed against the car behind them, Nancy couldn't look up. She didn't dare let go of Hagan.

"You okay, George?" was all she could say.

A feeling of relief shot through her when George replied, "Yup."

Nancy could feel Hagan's body jolt when he caught hold of Ned. She knew his job couldn't be easy—Ned weighed about one hundred and seventy pounds.

"Got him," the ride manager called, panting, then slowly hauled Ned up. Shouts of joy rose from the crowd below. Nancy stood up, threw her arms around Ned, and held tight.

"We made it," Ned said faintly. "I thought we might be goners for a minute there."

Nancy touched the cut on Ned's forehead gently. "What happened?" she asked.

"He hit the bar," George explained. "What a klutz, right?"

Ned laughed, and Nancy swung around and hugged George. "What about you? Are you okay?" she asked.

George smiled bravely and said, "I might have done something to my foot, but I'm not sure."

"We have to get these two to the hospital right away," Adriana broke in.

"I won't argue with that," Ned said, touching the wound on his forehead. "But tell me one thing—how do we get down?"

"Rand will lead the way," Adriana said firmly,

then touched the ride manager on the shoulder. "I don't know how to thank you for what you did."

Hagan only nodded before leading the way down the tracks.

Two hours later Nancy was still in the emergency room of Conklin Falls General Hospital, waiting for her friends to finish with their examinations. Adriana had just arrived, and the two of them were sitting on hard chairs, watching the late news on the television in the waiting area. A local news team had arrived during Ned and George's rescue and had taped the whole thing. Seeing the segment replayed before her eyes made Nancy's stomach twist.

Shots of Adriana conferring with the Conklin Falls sheriff and fire chief followed. They'd arrived just as the group made it down to safety. Then the reporter held the microphone to Adriana. "How do you explain this terrible accident," the man asked.

"I have no idea," she responded firmly. "My chief engineer checks everything every morning. We're extremely careful. The roller coaster was in top-notch condition."

The reporter went on to explain how Rand Hagan had heroically saved George and Ned with the help of Nancy and Adriana but then reminded the viewers about Freda Clarke's campaign against the park. "Are the rides at Riverfront safe for our kids?" he asked. "Only the state inspectors will be able to say for sure—but until then many believe that the park ought to be closed."

Adriana shook her head disgustedly and got up to switch off the television. "They made it sound as if Riverfront was old and dangerous," she said, "but the park is safe. I know it is."

"You should call my father first thing tomorrow morning," Nancy advised her.

"I definitely will," Adriana agreed. "I want to know what he thinks about keeping Riverfront open until the state inspectors arrive."

"When do you think they'll get here?" Nancy asked.

Adriana sighed. "They're notoriously slow, I'm afraid."

"In the meantime do you mind if I do some investigating?" Nancy asked.

The magician narrowed her eyes. "Are you thinking what I'm thinking—that the ride might have been sabotaged?"

Nancy nodded gravely, then said, "I want to check it out in the morning."

"Wonderful," Adriana replied. "I'll have Rand Hagan help you. He knows the Typhoon backward and forward. And I've called a staff meeting for tomorrow at one. Can you make it?"

"Sure," Nancy said.

"Rand worked for my uncle. He relied completely on the man, and I do, too," she explained. "Rand was one of the few people I kept on when I took over the place."

Just then Ned and George came through the swinging double doors of the emergency room. Ned's head was wrapped in a gauze bandage, and George's foot was encased in a plaster walking cast that came up to her ankle like a short boot.

"I can't believe it," she said, her face bright red. "I broke my big toe! They usually don't set them, but it was such a bad break they had to. This cast doesn't come off for almost a month. No running, swimming, or basketball! What am I supposed to do with myself?"

Nancy forced herself to keep a straight face, then said, "Don't worry, George. I'll keep you busy."

Her friend rolled her eyes.

"I'm just glad you're both able to walk out of here. How's your head, Ned?" Nancy asked.

"The doctor said I have a very slight concussion, but I feel okay," Ned replied.

"Come on. I'll take you guys home," Nancy said.

At that moment the swinging doors opened again, and a young woman in a lab coat emerged. She was holding a clipboard.

"I'm glad I caught you," the woman said. "I'm

30

Dr. McGill." Then she turned to Adriana and gave her a firm handshake. "I heard you were out here and wanted to meet you. I'm a really big fan."

Adriana smiled. "Thank you so much for taking care of my friends. I'm sure they were in very good hands."

"I hope you don't mind my asking," Dr. McGill said, "but I know that the children here at the hospital would love it if you could perform for them sometime."

Adriana clapped her hands together. "I'd love to!" she cried. "The sooner, the better."

"Why not on Wednesday morning?" Dr. McGill suggested.

"Perfect," said Adriana. "I'll be here at ten."

Dr. McGill thanked Adriana, gave a few more words of advice to George and Ned, then went back into the emergency wing. Nancy, Ned, George, and Adriana headed for the exit.

As they walked through the exit door, a petite woman came rushing up the front path toward them. She was wearing a red sweat suit and had a halo of brown curls that bobbed when she came to a halt in front of them.

"Not so fast, Adriana Polidori," the woman said, putting out a hand to stop the magician.

Adriana's green eyes widened in surprise.

"I saw what happened at Riverfront on the news," the woman began. "But it didn't surprise me. How could it, after what you did to my son?"

"For heaven's sake," Adriana said, "I did nothing to your son. That was last summer, before I came here. And his injury was ruled an accident. You know that as well as I do."

Nancy guessed that the woman must be Freda Clarke. She appeared to be in her thirties, and she had a pretty face, although it was now lined with tension.

For a second Freda drew back. "As you know, I disagree with the state inspectors' findings. And beyond that, Riverfront is an old, ill-maintained place—a hazard. Tonight's accident proves it," she insisted.

"That's ridiculous," Adriana replied.

Freda planted her feet in a wide, aggressive stance. "I'm not about to let this go. I want you to know that!"

Freda turned to George and Ned. "From what I saw on the news, you're lucky to be alive," she said. "Just think of what could have happened! I know that when you've had time to think things over, you'll agree to be witnesses."

"Witnesses?" Nancy echoed.

Freda Clarke faced Nancy now. "That's right," she replied firmly.

"What do you mean?" Ned asked.

"Against Adriana Polidori when I take her to court," Freda said. "It may be too late for my son, Chris, but it isn't too late for the rest of the children of Conklin Falls! It's my duty to protect them."

"Ms. Clarke—" Adriana began.

Freda didn't let her finish. "I'm putting you on notice, Adriana Polidori. I'm willing to fight you with everything I've got. And I'm going to win! I'm going to close Riverfront Park!"

Chapter

Four

"HOW DARE YOU bother these people at a time like this," Adriana said, straightening to her full height.

Freda moved forward, looking as if she was about to strike Adriana. Nancy stepped between the two women and put a calming hand on Freda's shoulder. The woman shrugged it off, then pulled a piece of paper and a pen out of her purse. She quickly wrote on it and handed it to Ned. "This is my address and phone number," Freda told him. "When you realize how close you came to losing your life—and that it was all because of Adriana Polidori—give me a call."

With that, Freda shot Adriana one last searing look, turned, and walked back through the parking lot to her car. George let out a low whistle.

34

"I can't believe that woman," Adriana said, her voice low. "She isn't being reasonable. She's trying to run me out of business."

"What exactly happened to her son?" Ned asked, fingering the paper with Freda's address. "It must be something pretty serious."

Adriana swallowed several times, obviously distraught. "He was thrown out of the Whirl-o-Looper. He broke his back."

"That's terrible," said Nancy, genuinely upset. "Was he wearing his safety harness?" she asked.

Adriana nodded. "Yes, but apparently it came unsnapped. Freda claims it broke loose, but there was no evidence of that. This was all cleared up by the inspectors before I came. There was even a hearing. But Freda wouldn't accept the ruling. She took on the park as something of a cause, even formed a citizens' group to pressure the city. The other members eventually lost interest, but Freda has persevered."

"How is her son now?" George asked.

Adriana sighed deeply. "I'm afraid he can't really walk. He uses braces and a wheelchair."

"Poor kid," Ned commented sympathetically.

"Uncle Nicos did everything he could to help the boy," Adriana went on. "But he couldn't wave a magic wand and make it all right. And it wasn't his fault," she insisted. "Now Freda's taking it out on me. She wants me to pay for what happened to Chris by closing down the park."

George reached out and put an arm around Adriana. "Don't worry," she said. "Nancy won't let her."

Nancy nodded. "No judge is going to make you shut down your park if the state inspectors decide that tonight's accident couldn't have been avoided—or if they find evidence of sabotage."

"Given what happened during the show, there *is* reason to suspect someone has it out for Riverfront," Ned said.

They remained silent for a minute as Ned's words sank in.

"We'll get to the bottom of it," Nancy said at last. Privately she didn't feel so confident, though. Finding a saboteur was like searching for the proverbial needle in the haystack, and for the moment Nancy had only one suspect—Freda Clarke. Somehow she didn't think the woman was capable of causing the accidents. But she *did* seem pretty unhinged by the whole Riverfront issue. Could she have hired someone at the park to act as her accomplice?

The night had turned chilly, and Nancy clutched her leather jacket around her as they walked back to their cars. They said their good-byes, with Nancy arranging to meet Adriana at the park for the staff meeting. Before that, she planned on examining the roller coaster.

By the time she dropped George off and took Ned back to his home, in Mapleton, it was almost two in the morning. Nancy slipped into her own house quietly so as not to awaken her father. She climbed the stairs, eager to fall into bed.

But as her head hit the pillow, Nancy's thoughts raced. She kept thinking of Freda Clarke and the intense expression on her face as she threatened to close down Adriana's park. The only question was—how far would she go?

Nancy slept until nine the next morning, and by the time she went downstairs for breakfast, her father had already left for the office. She knew Adriana would tell him what had happened when she called him later that morning.

Their housekeeper, Hannah Gruen, was visiting her sister's family in Chicago for the week, so Nancy fixed herself some toast and a bowl of cereal and sat down at the kitchen table. She grabbed the newspaper, which her father had left behind, from the counter and opened it up. She shook her head sadly when she saw the headline. "Disaster at Riverfront Park," it said. The story was enough to make parents keep their children away from Riverfront for good.

After reading the article, Nancy put down the paper and finished eating. In a grim mood she washed her dishes, grabbed her coat and shoulder bag, and left the house.

Driving through the fog and drizzling rain, Nancy planned her day. First, she wanted to follow up on the Freda Clarke angle. Ned had the woman's address, so it wouldn't be too hard to pay her a visit. Second, she intended to ask Adriana for a list of suspects—people inside the park who had access to the flame retardant tank as well as the expertise to sabotage the Typhoon.

It was almost eleven when she pulled into the parking lot at Riverfront. Through the mist Nancy could just make out the tall rides looming at the edge of the river bluffs. The night before, the park had been alive with lights, people, and activity, but now it resembled a ghost town. A fine frost had formed on the midway and crunched under Nancy's sneakers as she passed by the shuttered booths. Here and there Nancy spotted workers picking up trash from the night before. Otherwise, the park was quiet and empty.

When she reached the roller coaster, she noticed the yellow caution tape left behind by the police and guessed that they would be returning soon, along with the inspectors, to begin their investigation.

She slipped under the tape, passed near the operator's booth, and looked up. The derailed car was still dangling eerily. Nancy assumed it would have to stay that way until the state inspectors arrived.

She vaulted back onto the tracks and started the long climb, examining the rails and switching mechanisms as she went. Chances were that something on the track had caused the accident, Nancy guessed, and she intended to find out what it was.

When she reached the stalled train of cars at the summit, Nancy made her way to the front of the line. She bent down to scrutinize the spot where George and Ned's car had gone off the tracks. The rails were wet and slippery but intact, offering no evidence of what had caused the accident.

"You won't find what you're looking for up there," a voice called out. Nancy glanced behind her to see Rand Hagan making his way around the back cars.

The ride engineer was wearing gray overalls and the trademark bandanna around his neck again. When he smiled, there were crow's feet at the corners of his light blue eyes.

Nancy wiped her hands on her blue jeans. "I'm helping Adriana figure out what's happening here at the park," Nancy told him. "My name is Nancy Drew."

Hagan reached her side. "I remember from last night," he said simply.

"What did you mean when you said that I wouldn't find what I was looking for here?" Nancy asked him.

"Follow me," said Hagan.

He led the way back along the metal easement toward the second car in line. Nancy kept her hands on the guardrail as she went. When they reached the tail end of the second car, Hagan bent down and beckoned Nancy to do the same.

"First of all, take a look at the way these wheels

grip the track," he said. "See, it's not just one wheel. On each axle end there's a block with three wheels."

Nancy saw what he was describing. In each spot where she expected to find a wheel, there was instead a cluster of them. "Pretty impressive," she said.

"No matter what angle the cars bank at, these three wheels keep the cars securely in place," Hagan explained. "Now look here," he went on, pointing to the car's wheel block.

Nancy leaned closer. She saw that the whole wheel block was held to the axle by a massive nut, locked in place with a cotter pin about as thick as a knitting needle.

"Feel how secure that is," Hagan said. The apparatus was covered with grease, but when Nancy touched it, everything felt tight.

"That's the way it's supposed to be. I check every one of these blocks every morning. I did it yesterday. None were loose." Hagan rose, then took a rag from his back pocket and handed it to Nancy.

"So what you're saying is that somehow the block on the first car came loose," Nancy said as she wiped the grease off her fingers.

Hagan leaned against the car, his face still impassive. Nancy was sure he had more to tell her, but he was taking his time about it.

He looked toward the front car. "This morning, in the grass down there, I found one of the wheel blocks from the car that derailed," he finally said, pointing over the guardrail. "But I couldn't find the nut or the cotter pin. You'd need a metal detector for that."

"But if you checked the mechanism yesterday morning," Nancy replied, "how could the block have come off?"

Hagan tilted his head. "Only way would have been for someone to loosen the nut or take it off."

Nancy frowned.

"The car went over and over these tracks last night, and every time it went, the nut must have gotten a little bit looser. Eventually it and the cotter pin just flew off—"

"And the wheel went with them," Nancy finished for him, "which is why the car derailed and went over the side."

"Good thing the braking system worked," Hagan commented. "It's got electronic sensors, so if one of the trains doesn't pass a sensor when it's supposed to, the whole thing shuts down."

Nancy's mind was spinning. "So you think the ride could have been sabotaged?"

"Can't say." Hagan shrugged. "I'll tell you one thing, though. The state inspectors will go over this thing with a fine-tooth comb, but they're not going to find anything more than we did. They'll be able to say how the accident happened. But unless someone shows up with the nut and pin, there's no way they can prove it was sabotage."

41

Chapter

Five

Bᴜᴛ ᴛʜᴀᴛ ᴍᴇᴀɴs everyone will think that the ride isn't safe," Nancy gasped. There was a hollow feeling in the pit of her stomach. She could just imagine what Freda Clarke would make of this. The woman had already said that she planned to take Adriana to court over the accident involving her son.

"Sounds about right," Hagan agreed. "Adriana could have real trouble on her hands. An accident is much worse than an act of sabotage. Harder to explain."

Nancy's mind was working overtime now. Both Adriana and Hagan were sure that the ride was basically safe; Hagan had checked it himself. Then there was the question of the fire during Adriana's act. That definitely hadn't been an accident. There were too many suspicious things going on at Riverfront—too many "accidents."

Anyone who knew the park at all could have watched Adriana rehearse her act and figured out how to make it go wrong. It would have been easy enough to sneak into the prop room and fill the tank with kerosene. But what Nancy wanted to know was, who had the expertise to sabotage the Typhoon.

"Who knew enough about this ride to wreck it?" Nancy asked Hagan.

The engineer rocked on his heels. Scrutinizing Nancy carefully, he said, "Ride operator, couple of mechanics . . ."

Nancy saw a strange look suddenly flicker in his eyes. It was gone, though, before she could guess what it meant.

Hagan started easing around the last two cars of the train. Nancy followed. As she made her way down the tracks several paces behind him, a wind blew up and she shivered. She needed to get something warm inside her, but first she had to get more out of Hagan.

When they reached the ground, the two of them paused by the operator's booth.

"Look, Mr. Hagan," she said at last, "this is serious. I need the names of the people on your crew who'd be capable of weakening that wheel block," she insisted.

He kicked a stone, then looked at Nancy. "I

don't want to turn in anyone on my crew. Besides, I trust them—I hired them myself before the season started. After Nicos Polidori died, Adriana wanted to clear the decks, start all over. She told me to get the best people I could find, and I did."

"They may be good at their jobs," Nancy pressed, "but how do you know you can trust them?"

"I just do," he almost growled. Then he slumped a bit, his pale blue eyes wavering. "There is one guy. . . ." he began slowly.

"Yes," Nancy urged.

"I hate to even mention him—Benny Gotnick's his name. He used to work this ride and the Tunnel of Love, but Adriana fired him when she took over the park."

"Why?" Nancy asked. "What did he do?"

"It's what he didn't do," said Hagan. "Benny didn't work all that hard. Took long breaks, disappeared to smoke a cigarette, things like that."

Nancy frowned.

"He was a good old guy though—worked for Nicos for years, kind of a fixture around the place," Hagan went on reluctantly. "Of course, he gambled, ran up debts, goofed up pretty much. But he didn't have a mean bone in his body." He shrugged. "I guess he was pretty bitter when Adriana let him go."

"Bitter enough to want revenge?" Nancy asked.

Hagan stared blankly at her. "I don't know."

"Does he still live in Conklin Falls?" Nancy pressed.

"I've seen him around. Adriana should have his address in her files," Hagan replied.

It had started to drizzle again by now, so Nancy thanked Hagan for his help and walked back toward the auditorium where the staff meeting was scheduled to take place. When she reached the midway, she checked her watch. She was ten minutes late, so she started jogging, which warmed her up a bit.

She didn't look forward to telling Adriana the news about the roller coaster and that there was no way to prove it had been sabotaged from the evidence left behind. Still, she knew she had to. She also wondered what Adriana and her father had decided about keeping the park open until the state inspectors arrived. Given the bad press and Freda Clarke's threat, things were pretty grim.

Even so, Nancy had a small glimmer of hope— she now had two suspects, Freda Clarke and Benny Gotnick. For a minute she thought about Rand Hagan. He certainly knew enough about the Typhoon to sabotage it, but Adriana had said he was extremely reliable. What was more, he'd helped save Ned and George's lives, which struck Nancy as hardly the action of a saboteur.

When she reached the auditorium, she found one of the front doors unlocked and let herself in. She went through the empty lobby and into the theater, where Adriana was talking to her staff. Most of them were sitting on the stage, while a couple lounged in the front row. As Nancy moved down the aisle, she noticed Mikhail Grigov in a seat at the back.

"Nancy! There you are!" Adriana cried. The magician was wearing a pair of black trousers and a deep red sweater. "I'm sorry I didn't make it to the roller coaster. But did you see Rand there? I told him to meet you."

"Yes, I did." Nancy decided to wait to tell Adriana what she'd discovered until they were alone. "I'll talk to you afterward."

Adriana smiled and said, "Perfect." She called out to get the crew's attention and introduced Nancy to them. Then Adriana went around the room and called out their names. "That's Shauna and Glenn, our carpenters. André you've met. There's Maxine, the special effects expert, and Jenny, the pyrotechnician."

"I'll never remember you all," Nancy said, smiling as she sat down in the front row. "But I'll try." Then she turned to Adriana. "Has anyone figured out how the carpet got sprayed with kerosene last night?"

The group turned quiet and serious, and Nancy could see that they were upset.

Obviously uncomfortable, André spoke up at last. "I filled the tank the night before last. I had one of the new stagehands spray down the carpet before the show." He glanced over at Adriana. "I'm sorry. There were a million things to do. I never imagined someone would dump the No-Flame and substitute something else."

"Not your fault," Adriana told him. "You thought it was taken care of." She turned to Nancy. "We've discussed this pretty thoroughly. Someone from outside must have slipped in and made the switch. Maybe one of the new stage-hands."

"Do you have a list of their names?" Nancy asked.

"I'll get it for you," Adriana said.

"To be honest," Nancy began, "I'm looking for someone who not only had access backstage, but knew enough about the rides to sabotage the Typhoon."

For a long moment nobody said a word. Then André whistled. "I guess that lets all of us off the hook," he said.

"Of course," Adriana said. "We'd never doubt any of you."

"Besides," Jenny piped up, "none of us has a clue about the Typhoon. We all worked with Adriana on the road. Amusement park rides are definitely not our thing. Right, guys?"

The group murmured in agreement.

47

Nancy took a moment to digest the information, then focused on Adriana. "Do you remember a man named Benny Gotnick?" she asked.

Adriana's eyebrows shot up, but then she nodded. "I'm afraid I had to fire him when I took over. He was really hopeless, a terrible worker."

"Was he upset when you let him go?" Nancy continued.

Adriana sighed, pushed herself up on the apron of the stage, and crossed her long legs. "When I fired him, Benny promised me I'd regret it. I suppose he could have been serious."

Nancy was about to ask another question when a young man leaned out from the wings and said, "There's a phone call for you, Ms. Polidori. He says it's important."

"Who is it?" she called.

"Carson Drew," he replied.

Adriana smiled at Nancy. "I spoke to him a little while ago. He said he needed to make a few calls before he could get back to me," she explained, then got to her feet gracefully. "I'll make this as brief as I can." With that, she strode backstage.

Nancy turned to André. "How well do you know Rand Hagan?" she asked.

He smiled broadly. "Not that well. I met him when I came here two months ago. But without him, I don't know how this park would run. He's really good at his job—a little gruff, I guess, but smart."

"I played pool with him once at a place in Conklin Falls," the carpenter named Glenn mentioned, then laughed ruefully. "He's good at that, too."

Nancy chatted with the staff about life on the road with Adriana. They all clearly adored the woman and seemed happy to be at Riverfront. "I haven't stayed in one place for this long in years," Jenny commented.

Just then Adriana reappeared on the stage. She stopped walking for a moment and studied the group intently. Then she started moving toward them again. When she reached their circle, she stood still, her arms hanging at her sides.

After a long moment of silence, Adriana began speaking. "As you know I've been conferring with my lawyer, Carson Drew, about keeping the park open until the state inspectors come to check the Typhoon."

Her voice was hollow and lifeless. Nancy held her breath, waiting for Adriana to go on.

The magician hit her hands against her thighs. "Well, they're coming next week. But that may be a moot point."

Anger flashed through the magician's eyes. "Carson Drew just informed me that Freda Clarke has obtained an emergency restraining order to shut the park down. Effective immediately."

Chapter

Six

"WHAT?" Nancy asked. "How can she do that?"

Adriana turned to Nancy, her expression hard as steel. "Apparently, the first thing this morning, her lawyer petitioned the court for an injunction against the park. A hearing to determine whether we stay shut until the state inspectors show up next week is scheduled for the day after tomorrow. Until then we're forbidden to open."

"That's not fair," Glenn cried.

"Fair or not, it's the way things will be," Adriana replied bitterly. "There goes our first week's receipts."

"Adriana!" a deep voice boomed from behind them.

It was Grigov. Within seconds he'd come down the aisle, bounded onstage, and wrapped the magician in his arms. She crumpled against him, her strength clearly gone.

Holding her to him, he addressed the group. "There's nothing more to say. The meeting is over."

Adriana remained motionless as the members of her staff stood up and filed out of the auditorium. Nancy stayed in her seat in the front row, watching the two performers intently.

Grigov was stroking Adriana's hair in a way that made Nancy realize the two of them were more than professional partners. How deep did their attachment go? she wondered.

She cleared her throat to remind them that she was there, then stood and approached the stage.

Adriana drew away from Grigov and composed herself. "Forgive me," she said. "But this has all been too much."

"I understand," Nancy said softly.

"I'm going to fight this, though," she went on with fresh determination. "And when the state inspectors come, I know they'll vindicate me."

"I wanted to discuss that with you," Nancy began carefully, then went on to explain what Rand Hagan had shown her that morning.

Grigov sprang to life, his dark eyes flashing. "It's hopeless, my darling. You may suspect the ride was sabotaged, but you have no proof. You saw the paper this morning. The press is making you out to be a monster. You must give up this wretched plan of yours."

Adriana shot him an impatient look. "Absolutely not. Someone is trying to ruin this park, and when I find out who it is, I'll have him locked away for good." She smiled down at Nancy. "And I know someone who will help."

"Fine," Grigov spat out. "But when you're finished chasing ridiculous dreams, I'll be here, Adriana. My show leaves for Minneapolis in five days. Until then I plan to stay in Conklin Falls and do everything I can to convince you that I am right!"

"It won't do any good, Misha," she said calmly.

"Then, for the moment, I will say goodbye," Grigov told her.

Adriana's eyes followed him as he descended the steps at the side of the stage and strode back up the aisle. Then she turned to Nancy. "What is the next step in finding the culprit? Is there anything I can do to help you?" she asked.

"We've got two possibilities," Nancy said. "Either we're dealing with a vengeful ex-employee or someone else is trying to force you out. I need Benny Gotnick's address. But first, I'm going to pay a visit to Freda Clarke."

Adriana nodded. "Come with me and I'll get you Benny's file."

Ten minutes later Nancy left the auditorium with Benny Gotnick's address on a scrap of paper in her pocket. She was ravenously hungry and decided to stop to have a quick lunch. Then she'd call Ned and George.

Just as she was getting into her car, Nancy heard someone call her name. She looked up to see Mikhail Grigov striding toward her.

When he came closer, Nancy saw that his expression was furious. He grabbed Nancy by the arm and said, "You're not doing Adriana any favors by giving her all this so-called help of yours."

Nancy pulled free. "I don't appreciate being threatened," she said. "Why does it matter so much to you if Adriana keeps the park, anyway?"

Grigov pursed his lips. "We are old, old friends, Adriana and I." He shrugged, then backed off. "But I couldn't expect you to understand. All I know is this—Adriana belongs with me, not running this ridiculous park!"

With that, Grigov stormed away and got into a low black sports car that was parked on the far side of the lot. The car's engine roared to life, and Grigov's tires squealed as he pulled onto the road.

"Interesting," Nancy said out loud, watching him disappear. For a minute she recalled the way he'd held Adriana in the auditorium. Clearly he'd do anything for her. But did he want her to leave Conklin Falls so badly that he might actually sabotage her amusement park?

* * *

Nancy stopped at a diner and ordered a hamburger and soda, which she quickly ate. Then, after paying, she went out to make her calls at a telephone booth in the far corner of the parking lot. She reached Ned first. He said he had a bit of a headache but otherwise was fine. She got him to find the piece of paper Freda Clarke had given him and jotted down the woman's address.

The sound of cars and trucks whizzing by made it hard for Nancy to hear, and it had started to rain again.

"Look, Nancy," Ned said, "I'd like to see you tonight. After you're through at Benny Gotnick's and Freda Clarke's, I'm taking you out for a terrific dinner."

Tired and chilled as she was, the prospect filled her with pleasure. "Will you be feeling well enough?" she asked.

"Just talking to you makes me feel better," he said teasingly.

Nancy laughed. "Okay, you convinced me."

"I'll make reservations at Finian's and pick you up at eight," he said.

Nancy was smiling when she hung up. Finian's was one of the best restaurants in River Heights, which meant that Ned planned to make the evening special. She couldn't wait.

She called George next and found that her friend was in no pain but was seriously bored. Nancy told her everything that had happened and filled her in on her plans for the rest of the afternoon. George was only too happy to come along for the ride. Nancy told her she'd pick her up in an hour. She wanted to stop by her father's office first, because she had a few questions to ask him about Freda Clarke's injunction.

The rain was letting up a little when Nancy parked her car in the lot across from the building in downtown River Heights, where her father's law office was located. She nodded to the guard in the lobby, then got into a waiting elevator.

When she reached the office, the receptionist recognized her and called Carson Drew's secretary to let her know that Nancy was there.

As the woman put down the phone, she said, "Your father will be right out."

Nancy thanked her and was just about to sit down when Carson Drew stuck his head out the door.

"Nancy, honey! It's great to see you. What a surprise," he said. He hugged her, then ushered her down the long corridor that led to his office.

"I'm really sorry to bother you, Dad," she said as they went. "I just need to know what's going on with Freda Clarke's injunction. I can't believe that she managed to get it so fast."

Carson's office was lined with bookcases and furnished with mahogany chairs and a leather couch. Behind his desk was a large window that overlooked Courthouse Square.

He closed the door behind them, then sat down at his desk and propped his feet up on its paper-cluttered surface.

Nancy sat down in one of the chairs across from his desk.

"As you can see," he said, "I'm overwhelmed with work." He grinned at his daughter. "But I'm never too busy to see you. Especially when I'm involved in a case that requires your detective skills."

"That's exactly why I'm here," Nancy said. She started to explain what she'd learned that morning at the roller coaster, but her father stopped her.

"Adriana told me." He rubbed his jaw.

Nancy gazed out the window for a minute, then said, "Things don't look good for her, do they, Dad?"

He sighed. "I'll tell you one thing. Freda Clarke's got one sharp lawyer." He proceeded to explain how Freda's legal counsel had managed to get the injunction against the park. Then he leaned back in his chair and shook his head. "I'm afraid that after the incident last night, I'm going to have a tough time making a case for her at the hearing on Thursday."

"What happens when the state inspectors make a determination about what really caused the accident?" Nancy asked.

"I imagine that there will be another hearing about the park's long-range future," he replied.

Nancy hit her fist on her thigh. "I *know* someone's trying to sabotage the park! The things that have been happening there are just too weird."

"I agree," Carson said. "But unless you can prove that there's been sabotage, I've got nothing to go on, I'm afraid." He picked up a pen and started twisting it between his thumb and fingers. "I'd really like to save Riverfront, though—for Adriana's sake."

"What do you know about Freda Clarke? I plan to pay her a call," Nancy said.

He raised his eyebrows. "Only that she's been after Riverfront since her son Chris's accident. And that she's got money and power behind her."

Nancy frowned. "What do you mean?"

"She's divorced and her fiancé is a very prominent businessman in Conklin Falls. He used to be on the city council there, as I recall. Vince Garraty's his name. He owns a big garbage hauling and disposal plant just south of town."

"Interesting," Nancy murmured.

"Mind you, I don't think he cares all that much about the park. I get the feeling he's just humoring Freda," Carson went on.

Just then the phone rang, and he grabbed it. "Yes, hello," he said.

Nancy listened as he made arrangements to pick up the person he was talking to at eight-thirty that night. When he put the phone down several minutes later, he raised his eyes to Nancy. "I've got a business dinner tonight, I'm afraid. Don't wait up for me."

Nancy nodded.

"We'll talk tomorrow morning. I want to know what you find out from Freda. It could help me at the hearing," he said.

After Nancy had swung by George's house to pick her up, the weather had become almost mild and the sun was peeking out from behind the clouds. At a stoplight Nancy took off her jacket and rolled down the window. Then she spoke to George. "Something kind of weird happened when I was at my father's office," she began.

"An escaped convict your father put away showed up with a gun and tried to kidnap you, right?" George teased, bending down to scratch the skin just beneath the top of her cast. "This thing itches like crazy."

Nancy rolled her eyes. "I'm serious, George. I was sitting in his office and he got a call. He acted like it was a client, but it sounded more like a date."

"Get real, Nancy," George replied. "Your dad's a good-looking guy. There's no reason he shouldn't have a date or two."

Nancy felt herself blushing. "Of course not. But like I said, it was strange."

After a twenty-minute drive up the parkway,

Nancy took an exit that led to quiet, tree-lined streets. George navigated from a map in her lap, and they quickly found Freda Clarke's house on a block of well-kept homes.

"This is it," George said as Nancy pulled to a stop in front of a white bungalow.

After parking the car, Nancy and George approached the house. Four wide steps led up to the front porch, and a sturdy plywood panel had been nailed over them, turning half the staircase into a ramp.

George walked up the steps beside Nancy, and Nancy rang the doorbell.

A minute later the door swung open and a voice asked, "May I help you?"

"Chris Clarke?" Nancy asked when she saw the young boy standing at the door.

"That's me. Who are you?"

"My name is Nancy Drew. This is my friend, George Fayne. Is your mother home?"

Chris peered at them from behind the screen door. Nancy guessed he was about twelve years old. He was a cute, sandy-haired boy with braces on his legs and was supporting himself on a pair of metal crutches. Nancy could see that he was considering his answer before saying, "Uh, no, she's out shopping. She won't be back for a while."

"Could you tell her we stopped by?" Nancy suggested.

"Sure," Chris said. Nancy was about to turn to go when Chris asked, "Is there something I can help you with?"

Nancy could tell from the eagerness in his voice that he wanted company. "Maybe there is," she said. "We want to ask your mom some questions about your accident last summer, but as long as you're here, maybe you can answer them."

Now Chris seemed a bit doubtful. "I don't know," he said. "Maybe I shouldn't talk to you." He acted disappointed. Then he noticed George's cast. "Hey, how did you hurt your foot?"

"I was on the roller coaster at Riverfront Park last night," she answered.

"Really?" he cried. "That must have been scary! And all you hurt was your foot?"

"My big toe, actually," George explained.

"That's not so bad," Chris consoled her. "It'll heal in no time." The boy looked behind him and then unlocked the screen door. "Why don't you come in? My mom should be back soon."

He led them into the living room, where the television was blaring, and eased himself into a nearby wheelchair.

"Grab a seat," Chris said, pointing to the couch. He flicked off the television with a remote control. "You guys were at Riverfront last night? Boy, do I miss that place!"

"You do?" George asked, a bit surprised.

"Sure—I always loved going there," he said.

"But isn't that where you were hurt?" George pressed.

"I guess." He looked away sheepishly. "But maybe that wasn't all the park's fault."

"What do you mean?" Nancy asked.

Now Chris really looked embarrassed. "I was in the Whirl-o-Looper with my friends, and we were horsing around. I had my safety belt kind of loose so I could reach over and take a poke at this guy, Teddy. But the belt came all the way off, and I got thrown around in the car."

"And that's how you got hurt?" George asked in amazement.

"Yeah," Chris replied, staring down into his lap.

"Did you tell your mom that?" Nancy pressed.

"Yeah," he said, "but she's convinced the strap shouldn't have come undone."

From the doorway there came a stunned gasp. Nancy and George whirled around to see a woman standing in the entrance to the living room, her arms full of packages. It was Freda Clarke. Beside her was a tall man, muscular and broad shouldered.

"I recognize you!" Freda cried, dropping her packages on the floor. "You're that friend of Adriana Polidori's. You were at the hospital last night."

At the mention of Adriana's name, the man strode across the living room and grabbed Nancy by the shoulder.

"Get out," he growled, "before I throw you out!"

Chapter

Seven

THE MAN'S GRIP on Nancy's shoulder felt like a powerful vise. She squirmed, but he wouldn't let go, so she elbowed him hard in the stomach.

"Ummph," he cried, releasing her and staggering backward several steps.

Nancy straightened up, and George came to her side. "You could have at least asked us nicely," George shot at him.

Nancy turned to Freda. "Listen," she said, searching for a way to get the woman to simmer down and talk, "we both want the same thing."

"We do?" Freda was obviously skeptical.

"Yes." Nancy took a deep breath. "Riverfront Park isn't safe, that's clear." At this, Freda smiled, and Nancy went on. "I want it to be safe, and so do you. But you think the only way for that to happen is to shut the place down. I think we need to find out what's going on there, so Adriana can keep it open."

"This is hogwash," the man cut in. Nancy studied him for a second. His face was slightly tanned, and he wore jeans, a sports jacket, and loafers.

"Just a minute, Vince," Freda said. "Let's hear what she has to say."

"You're Vince Garraty?" Nancy asked.

"Yes," he replied curtly, "Freda's fiancé. What's it to you?"

"Nothing," Nancy said mildly.

"She just likes to know the names of the people who assault her," George snapped.

From his wheelchair, Chris giggled softly, making Nancy suspect that the boy didn't like Vince very much.

"Get on with it," Vince growled.

Nancy smiled as sweetly as she could under the circumstances. "I just want to talk about the accidents, because—well, there's a chance the park's being sabotaged."

"That's ridiculous," Freda cried, her eyes sparkling. "The accidents are being caused by negligence. Nothing more and nothing less. Her uncle mismanaged the place, and now Adriana is. It's a hazard, and we all know it." Freda stared hard at Chris. "Aren't we proof enough?"

Nancy reached toward Freda and said, "Ms. Clarke, I know how much you and Chris have suffered, but—"

"Look," Vince lashed out, "this is going no-where. The whole thing will be decided in court." He strode to the door and held it open. "I'm sick of you pestering Freda. I want you out—now—and I don't want to ask again!"

Nancy could tell they wouldn't get much further with Freda and Vince. She walked out the front door with George close behind.

"That was asking?" George said as they headed toward the car. "I'd hate to see what happens when he tells someone to do something."

Nancy noticed a truck parked at the curb with the words Garraty Hauling and Disposal, Inc., 10900 River Bluff Road, 232-7961 painted on the side. There were smaller letters below the company name and address. " 'Where there's no such thing as trash,' " Nancy read aloud.

"Nice," George commented dryly.

Once they were in Nancy's car, George said, "That didn't go too well, did it?"

"Actually, better than you might think." Nancy started up the engine. "Chris as much as admitted that his accident wasn't all the park's fault, and I got a chance to meet Vince Garraty."

"What a delight!" George replied, then buckled her seat belt and grabbed the map. "Where to next?" she asked.

"Find this street on the map," Nancy said, handing her the slip of paper with Benny Gotnick's address on it.

"Right," George responded.

Ten minutes later they were parked in front of a dilapidated little house on a seedy street in Conklin Falls. The paint on the house was chipping, and the tiny yard was overgrown with weeds.

"I don't see a car. Do you think he's in there?" George asked. "The place looks almost abandoned."

"Only one way to find out," Nancy replied. "Stay here. I'll be right back." She got out of the car and made her way through the weeds to the front door.

There was no bell, so she pounded on the door. After a while she turned back to George and gave a shrug. She tried the door. It was locked. She knocked again, just to make sure, then reached into her bag for her lockpicking kit.

"Looking for Benny?" she heard someone call.

Nancy swung around and saw a middle-aged man in khaki pants and a faded flannel shirt emerge from the house next door. She quickly tucked her kit back in her shoulder bag.

"He's at work," the man said affably. "But you could catch him after six or so."

"Great," Nancy replied. "I'll come back." Then she started down the cracked walk but, on second thought, stopped. "You don't happen to know where he works, do you?" she asked, smiling. "I'm the daughter of an old friend of his, and I kind of wanted to surprise him."

"Sure," the man said. "Garraty Hauling, just south of town."

Nancy's eyes widened, but she kept her voice level. "Thanks. I'll try there," she said.

When she got back to the car and pulled away from the curb, she let out a long breath. "Did you hear that, George?"

Her friend nodded.

Nancy checked her watch. It was almost five-thirty. "Up for a little more work before we call it a day?" she asked.

"What do you have in mind?" George asked.

"I'd like to check out Garraty's place—nose around, see if we can find Benny, that sort of thing. I remember the address from the truck. River Bluff Road. Benny's neighbor said it's just south of town."

"Not a bad idea," George said. "You know, it really is weird that Benny works for Vince. Do you think it could have any connection to the case?"

"I don't know," Nancy replied. "But I definitely want to avoid running into Vince. Somehow, I don't think he'd welcome us with open arms."

"I know what you mean," George agreed.

As it turned out, Garraty Hauling and Disposal was about half a mile north of Adriana's amusement park. A sign pointed down a dirt drive that led to a gate and a chain link fence surrounding the complex. There wasn't a guard, so Nancy drove right into the lot.

"Let's just cruise around," Nancy said, slowing the Mustang to five miles an hour. At one side there was a big garage with two Garraty trucks pulled up to loading bays. Next door was a prefabricated building with a sign indicating that the company's main office was inside.

Nancy steered around the garage. Behind it was another parking lot, bigger than the first, with several dump trucks parked in it. At the back Nancy noticed a tanker. On its side, in bold letters, were the words Warning—Toxic Waste.

At the far side of the lot was an enormous warehouse with scores of steel drums stacked outside. The whole place seemed to be deserted, probably because it was after five, Nancy surmised.

"I doubt we'll find Benny around now," George said.

"You're right," Nancy answered. She turned the car around. "But maybe I'll stop in at the office, just to be sure."

"You're a brave soul, Nancy Drew," George joked.

Nancy parked in front of the office building and was just about to get out when George hissed, "Stop!"

Through the windshield, Nancy could see Vince Garraty coming out the front door with a briefcase in his hand. She and George ducked, their heads close together on the front seat. "I guess he didn't stick around at Freda's," George whispered.

Only when they heard Vince start up his car and drive away did they get up.

"That was a close one," Nancy said, grinning.

George just shook her head.

Nancy decided to take the scenic route, along River Bluff Road, back to River Heights. The parkway was more direct, but River Bluff was prettier, especially south of the amusement park.

As she drove, Nancy thought about the Benny Gotnick–Vince Garraty connection. Could the two of them be working together? she wondered. It made a certain amount of sense. Vince had definitely been hostile to her at Freda's.

Her father had said that Vince didn't really care all that much about closing down Riverfront. He was only humoring his fiancée. Would he engage in sabotage for her sake though? He was a respected businessman with a good deal to lose. It didn't seem likely.

Benny was the key, she decided. The next day she'd track him down no matter what.

Gradually her thoughts strayed to her date that night with Ned. It would be wonderful to be alone with him. A long-distance relationship wasn't easy, but Ned and Nancy were trying their best to make it work.

"Earth to Nancy!" George called out.

Nancy shook herself out of her reverie. "Sorry, George. What?"

George laughed. "Nothing in particular. I just wanted to make sure you were still there."

For the next ten minutes Nancy kept her mind on the road. Below and to her right, the river wound its way south to River Heights. The road meandered through the woods, then curved back toward the cliffs above the river. A gravel shoulder and guardrail were all that separated it from a two-hundred-foot drop. After a few miles, Nancy realized that the car behind her was perilously close. She sped up, and so did the other car. When she slowed down again, the other car remained close behind.

"What's wrong?" George asked.

"I think someone's tailing us," Nancy answered.

Then, with a screech of tires, the black sports car sped up and started to zoom around them on the left, forcing Nancy to steer the Mustang toward the gravel shoulder at the right.

"What a jerk!" George said.

The windshield was tinted dark so Nancy couldn't see the driver as the sports car started to pass.

All at once the black car veered toward Nancy's Mustang, ramming her front left fender. Nancy clutched the steering wheel, but the Mustang jolted and swerved wildly.

As the black car pulled past them, Nancy

fought to straighten the wheels of the Mustang. It was too late. The front end of the Mustang hit the gravel shoulder and skidded toward the guard-rail.

Nancy saw a slice of the river shimmer before her.

George screamed, "We're heading right for the edge!"

Chapter

Eight

Nancy desperately held on to the wheel, trying to control the Mustang. She hit the metal guardrail anyway and felt it give way.

"Look out!" George screamed.

Then without warning Nancy felt the wheels bite into the rough shoulder of the road. The Mustang came out of the skid! Nancy turned the wheel to the left until the car was straight and reentered the lane.

Fifty feet up the road was a scenic lookout, so Nancy slowed down and pulled in, her heart pounding, her hands almost welded to the wheel.

Both girls sat in stunned silence for several minutes.

"Are you okay?" Nancy finally asked George.

George let out a deep breath. "Fine, considering that a maniac just tried to kill us."

Nancy opened the car door and looked back up the road, but the sports car had long since disappeared around a bend. "You didn't happen to see the license plate number, did you?"

George shook her head. "I could make a stab at the first few letters. But it all happened so fast."

"I know," Nancy agreed. "And the car's windows were tinted, so I couldn't see the driver at all." Frustrated, she hit the steering wheel with the palm of her hand. "Well, I guess I'd better get out and take a look at the damage."

The front left fender was pretty banged up, but the car was still operable.

"We were lucky," George said as she came around from the passenger side and bent down to inspect the damage. George ran her hand over the dent. "Well, whoever the driver was, he lost some paint," she said slowly.

Nancy leaned in close and scrutinized the scrape mark. George was right. There was a trace of black paint over the dented blue metal.

Suddenly she sprang up. "I know I've seen a black sports car someplace recently," she said, leaning her hands against the hood. "Where was it?"

George remained silent so that Nancy could concentrate.

Then a dark look passed over Nancy's face. "Mikhail Grigov!"

"Adriana's old partner?" George exclaimed. "But why would he try to run us off the road?"

"I told you how he threatened me in the parking lot at Riverfront, didn't I?" Nancy reminded her friend. "That's where I saw his car, and it was definitely a sporty black number—European, I think."

"So you've got another suspect now," George remarked.

"Yes." Nancy sighed. "And it's also pretty clear that someone wants me off the case."

"Don't you think we'd better go back into Conklin Falls and report this to the sheriff?" George asked.

Nancy nodded in agreement. "I've got some questions I want to ask him about the roller coaster accident anyway."

The two friends got back into the car and headed into town. Within ten minutes they had found the headquarters of the sheriff's department, a two-story brick building on the main street, right next to the courthouse. The deputy on duty directed them to Sheriff Pulaski's office.

The sheriff rose from behind his desk as Nancy and George came through the door. He was a compact, fit man of about fifty or so, whose brown hair was shot through with gray. Nancy immediately recognized him from the television news segment the night before. She quickly introduced herself and George, and Pulaski shook their hands. He took a seat behind his desk, while Nancy and George sat down opposite him.

"What can I do for you?" the sheriff asked.

Nancy got right to the point. She briefly explained her involvement in the case at Riverfront Park and then told him about being run off the road by a man in a car that looked like the one owned by Adriana's ex-partner.

The sheriff instantly turned businesslike and pulled a report form out of his desk. "So you figure it was this Mikhail Grigov character," the sheriff said. "Did you actually see him behind the wheel?"

"No, the glass was tinted so dark that I couldn't make a positive identification," Nancy said.

"Did you get the license number?" Pulaski asked.

Nancy bit her lower lip. "Not exactly." On the way back into Conklin Falls, George had been able to remember the first two letters of the plate. Nancy gave them to Pulaski now. "I realize that's not a lot to go on."

"No, it isn't," the sheriff agreed. He leaned back in his chair and stretched his arms above his head. "And I really don't see what Grigov stands to gain by threatening you or sabotaging Riverfront—*if* it's been sabotaged."

Nancy told the sheriff about the roller coaster's missing wheel block.

"Sounds like an accident to me—" He ran his hand through his hair, which sprang up into a cowlick at his touch.

George stared pointedly at Nancy, silently

communicating a thought Nancy shared—that Pulaski wasn't going to be much help to them.

"Between you and me, I don't think there's any real mystery here, Nancy. But the state inspectors will figure it all out," he went on. He grinned up at her. "Why don't you give it a rest?"

Nancy was starting to get frustrated. "I realize the evidence is sketchy," she began intently, "but there's definitely trouble at Riverfront, and I'm going to get to the bottom of it. In the meantime would you file a report about what just happened to us on River Bluff Road?"

Pulaski seemed taken aback by Nancy's determination. He rubbed the side of his nose and said, "Right. And we'll see if we can track down Grigov, bring him in for questioning, that sort of thing."

"Thank you," Nancy said firmly, then stood up. She gave the sheriff her number at home, then she and George left his office.

"I think you might have won him over at the end there, Nan," George said as they got back into the Mustang.

Nancy sighed and started the ignition. "Let's hope so."

"I just have one favor to ask," said George.

"What's that?"

"Can we take the parkway back to River Heights?" George asked. "I think I've had enough adventure for one day!"

* * *

At eight o'clock that night Nancy bounded down the carpeted stairs of her house to answer the doorbell. Her father had gone straight from his office to his dinner appointment, so Nancy was home alone.

When she reached the foyer, she caught a glimpse of herself in the mirror and nodded in approval at her flowing scoop-necked dress. Her friend Bess Marvin had helped her pick it out. Its ivory- and rose-colored flowers against an emerald green background set off her reddish blond hair perfectly. She smoothed the dress over her hips, then threw open the door to Ned, leaning casually against the frame.

"What a babe!" he exclaimed to tease her, then stepped over the threshold and put his arms around her. He tilted her chin up and looked into her eyes. "I've been waiting for this all day!"

He kissed her lips gently, and Nancy caught the lapel of his jacket between her thumb and forefinger. "You don't look so bad yourself—for a guy with a dent in his head," she joked back.

Ned was wearing a trim dark blue suit, a white shirt, and an expensive Italian tie Nancy's father had given him for Christmas. His broad shoulders filled out the jacket perfectly, and the colors of the tie set off his deep brown eyes.

"Thanks a lot," he replied good-naturedly.

Nancy reached up and touched the bandage on his forehead. "Actually, this makes you look even

77

more handsome—kind of like a pirate. Do you feel okay?" she asked.

"Good as new," he replied, then grabbed her hand. "Come on, Nan. We've got reservations at eight-thirty, and I don't want them to give our table away to somebody else."

Nancy reached back to the coatrack beside the door for her wrap, then locked the door and went down the walk arm in arm with Ned.

On the way to Finian's, Nancy told her boyfriend about what had happened that day. When she got to the part about being run off River Bluff Road, Ned's brow furrowed.

"I want you to be careful," he said. "This case is getting dangerous."

Nancy sighed. "I know. I keep thinking about the knife I saw in Grigov's hand when I was talking to Adriana in her dressing room last night."

Ned widened his eyes. "He had a knife?"

"Didn't I tell you?" Nancy said. "He's a professional knife thrower. His stage name is Sabre the Blademaster."

"Oh, boy!" Ned exclaimed. "I thought he was kind of weird when I met him. Possessive of Adriana, you know?"

Nancy frowned. "There's definitely something between the two of them, but I haven't had a chance to ask Adriana about it. Even though she doesn't seem to take him completely seriously, I get the feeling that they're romantically involved.

But it could be a touchy subject, if you know what I mean."

Ned nodded. "So, besides Grigov, who are your suspects now?" he wanted to know. "Freda Clarke?"

"I guess I've got to keep her on the list, even though I doubt she'd do anything illegal. I'm not so sure about her fiancé, Vince Garraty, though," Nancy said. "He was definitely hostile when I met him at Freda's house. And then there's Benny Gotnick."

"It's pretty interesting that Benny works for Vince, wouldn't you say?" Ned asked.

"No kidding," Nancy agreed. "I'm going back to his place tomorrow. If he's not there, I'll check out the premises."

"Breaking and entering again?" Ned teased as he pulled into Finian's and parked. "It's getting to be a real habit with you."

Nancy laughed.

The maître d' greeted them just inside the door. He led them through the dining room to their table. Finian's was a beautiful restaurant, one of Nancy's favorites. The walls were oak paneled and covered with oil paintings. The floor was carpeted in deep, plush wool, and the tables were set with fine china and crystal.

Their table was off to the side of the main dining room, and Nancy sat facing Ned with her back to the entrance. After they ordered their appetizers she leaned across the table to hold

Ned's hand. "This place is so romantic. Being here with you is the greatest, Nickerson."

Ned smiled back at her, but then his expression turned quizzical. Nancy noticed that he was staring past her. "What is it?" she asked.

"You might not be the only Drew who thinks Finian's is romantic," he said.

"What do you mean?" Nancy asked.

"Your father just walked in."

"My dad!" Nancy exclaimed. "But he said he had a business appointment."

"This doesn't look like a business appointment to me," said Ned. "This looks like a date."

Nancy turned in her seat to peer over her shoulder. Indeed, her father, dressed in a charcoal gray suit, had just entered the restaurant. His eyes were sparkling, and he was smiling broadly. Nancy couldn't remember the last time she'd seen him look so handsome—or so happy.

It was only when Carson Drew stepped forward that Nancy saw what she assumed was the reason for her father's joy. With him was a striking woman, dressed in an off-the-shoulder red dress, her black hair piled glamorously on top of her head.

Nancy's breath caught in her throat as she recognized the woman. It was Adriana Polidori!

Chapter

Nine

Nancy couldn't believe her eyes. "My father," she whispered, "and Adriana Polidori!"

"What's wrong with that?" Ned asked. They both watched as Carson squired Adriana through the restaurant.

Then Nancy turned back to the table. "She's a client for one thing," she said, and took a big swallow of ice water.

Ned raised an eyebrow but said nothing.

"You know I don't mind my father dating." She toyed with a lock of her hair. "It's just that things can become confusing when business and —personal relationships get mixed up," she finished a little weakly.

Ned shot her a look. "Keep it down, Nancy. They're headed this way."

Carson stopped dead in his tracks as he passed

their table. Nancy could tell from the embarrassed expression on his face that her father wasn't any more comfortable with the situation than she was. She decided to do her best to make him feel at ease.

"Dad, what a wonderful surprise!" she said, standing up to give her father a peck on the cheek. "You look gorgeous," she said, turning to Adriana.

The magician smiled and glanced up at Carson. "Thank you. Your father said this was one of the best restaurants in River Heights and that I simply had to try it. I told him that as long as we were conducting business, it might as well be pleasurable, too."

Carson nervously adjusted his tie, and Nancy's gaze darted back and forth between them. Maybe it was just a dinner appointment with an important client, she thought. Maybe there wasn't anything going on between them. Still, Nancy's instincts were on the alert. If her father got too close to Adriana, he might lose some of his judgment about her case.

"We'd better take our table," Carson said.

"Have a great time," Ned put in. "The shrimp cocktail's terrific!"

For the rest of their meal, Nancy tried to keep her eyes off her father's table. Every time she looked up, though, it seemed as if Carson and Adriana were laughing and gazing into each other's eyes.

When it was time for dessert, Ned ordered a slice of Mississippi mud pie. The waiter brought it with two forks.

Nancy took a bite of the moist chocolate dessert. "This is incredible!" she said, but her mind was still focused on her father and Adriana. "I want to ask Adriana about Grigov. But something tells me that now is not the time."

Ned frowned. "You may be right—especially if there really is something between the two of them."

"And I've got to tell my dad what happened in the car today. The fact that somebody who drives a black sports car wants me off the case could have a bearing on the way he defends Adriana at her hearing," Nancy said.

"This *is* pretty sticky," Ned replied thoughtfully. "Do you think he knows about Grigov?"

"Adriana wouldn't be dating my dad at the same time she's involved with her ex-partner—would she?" Nancy asked.

"I don't get the feeling that she'd do that sort of thing," Ned responded. "But I don't know her all that well."

"Neither do I," Nancy said.

On their way out, Ned and Nancy stopped by her dad's table to say goodbye. The waiter had just taken away Carson and Adriana's entrée plates.

Adriana stretched back in her chair, holding on to its oak arms. "Listen, Nancy," she said, "something happened late today that I think you ought to know about."

"What?" Nancy asked.

"I got a call from a realtor in Conklin Falls— Larry Matthews is his name. He has a client who wants to buy Riverfront."

Nancy narrowed her eyes.

"I told him that I'm not interested in selling, of course," Adriana went on. "But I thought the timing was a little strange."

"I'd call it downright suspicious," Nancy's father put in.

Ned looked at Carson. "You mean that maybe someone's been rigging these accidents at the park to drive down the selling price?" Ned asked.

"It's a distinct possibility," Carson replied.

"Did you get the client's name?" Nancy asked.

"Unfortunately, Matthews wouldn't say," Adriana answered.

"What do you think the buyer has in mind for the place?" Nancy queried her dad.

"Well," he said slowly, removing his linen napkin from his lap and laying it on the table, "it's a prime riverfront lot. I could see a shopping mall there or a condominium complex."

"That's one more thing I've got to do tomorrow then—persuade Larry Matthews to tell me who his client is," Nancy said.

Before Ned and Nancy left, Adriana reminded them about the magic show the next day at Conklin Falls General Hospital.

"I'm counting on you to be there," Adriana said. "Especially since my other performance came to such a premature end."

"I wouldn't miss it," Nancy told the magician, then tried to lighten up a bit. "See you at home, Dad," Nancy said. She shook her finger at him mischievously. "Now, don't be out too late."

Carson laughed. "I won't."

"That was nice of you to joke with your father," said Ned as they were leaving Finian's.

Nancy sighed. "You've got to admit, it was an awkward situation."

"It'll all get sorted out," Ned assured her.

They got into Ned's car and headed back to Nancy's house. On the way Nancy and Ned plotted strategy for the next day. She would pick up George in the morning and head up to the hospital to catch Adriana's show. Ned said he'd meet them there. Then Nancy would devote the rest of the day to hunting down Benny Gotnick and seeing whether she could get any information out of the realtor, Larry Matthews.

Ned pulled to a stop in front of Nancy's house. "What about the Grigov angle?"

Nancy peered out into the darkness. "Sheriff Pulaski said he'd question him," she commented. "I guess I'm counting on him to find Grigov. If he doesn't, I'll have to confess my suspicions to Adriana and see how she reacts." A troubling idea crossed Nancy's mind.

"What is it?" Ned asked, picking up on her thoughts.

"I don't know how to explain it," Nancy said, trying to make sense of what was bothering her. "I guess I'm worried that Adriana might get upset if I start accusing Grigov. And what if my father gets in the middle of all this?"

"Don't worry, Nan," Ned said. "As I said, everything will work out." Then he gave her a long, lingering kiss good night.

"Mmmm, that smells good," Nancy said as she entered the kitchen the following morning. Carson Drew was cooking breakfast. "Hey—french toast!" she noted happily. "And on a Wednesday. I hope you didn't forget to put some cinnamon in the batter."

"Of course not," he said with a smile. "I'm the one who taught you to make french toast, remember?" Carson reached out to give Nancy a hug. "I could see you were a little upset last night, Nancy. I'm sorry I didn't tell you I was having dinner with Adriana."

Nancy stepped back from her father and smiled. "It's okay. But I guess I *was* a little surprised."

"And worried," Carson added. He turned back to the stove and flipped two slices of french toast that were cooking in a large frying pan.

Nancy sat down at the kitchen table. "Maybe." She paused. "Dad, has Adriana mentioned anything to you about her former partner, Mikhail Grigov?"

Carson frowned. "Only that he's been trying very hard to get her to go back on the road."

Nancy paused, searching for the right words. "He's in Conklin Falls this week. He actually warned me not to help Adriana get to the bottom of the accidents. He thinks that Riverfront is cursed."

Carson laughed. "That's putting it a little strongly, I'd say."

Nancy could tell that her father had no suspicions whatsoever about Adriana and Grigov, and it concerned her.

She proceeded to tell him about the incident on River Bluff Road and the fact that Sheriff Pulaski was going to question Grigov about it.

"Why didn't you mention it to Adriana last night?" Carson asked.

Nancy played with her fork for a minute. "It just didn't seem the right time," she finally replied. "But I *will* talk to her about it today."

"Do that," Carson said, bringing a plate piled high with french toast to the table and sitting down. "Now, dig in before it gets cold."

As they ate, they chatted about the upcoming hearing. When they finished, Carson pushed his chair back. "I'd better get to the office," he said. "I've got a busy day."

"I'll do the dishes," Nancy replied. "And thanks for breakfast. It was great!"

"Anything for my girl," he said, kissing her on the forehead as he passed by.

Half an hour later Nancy and George pulled into the parking lot at Conklin Falls General Hospital. Ned was waiting for them at the front door.

When they were inside the hospital, a nurse directed them to the cafeteria in the children's wing. It had a low, paneled ceiling and a bank of windows that overlooked the parking lot. At the far end was a platform with several hospital room dividers in front of it.

Folding chairs had been set up in front of it. The audience, composed of young patients and their parents, was already seated and waiting.

Nancy and her friends were about to sit when a voice called out. "Hey, George, over here!" They looked around, and George spotted Chris Clarke sitting in a wheelchair parked across the aisle.

"Hi, Chris," she greeted him. "Considering who's performing, I'm surprised your mom let you come here today."

"Aw, she doesn't know about the magic show. She just dropped me off for my regular physical therapy session. Why don't you pull a chair over and sit with me?"

George smiled at Nancy and Ned. "How can I resist? See you two after the show."

Just then Dr. McGill stood up in front of the audience. "I want to thank you all for being here," she said. "And now, without further ado, I am proud to present the great Adriana Polidori!"

Two nurses pulled apart the dividers, and Adriana stepped out. She was wearing a classic magician's costume consisting of a top hat, tails, and trousers, but the dressy men's clothes were cut to fit her figure, and she looked strikingly feminine. She smiled warmly at the audience.

"You know," she said, leaning toward them and winking conspiratorially, "I don't get a chance to work with a small audience much anymore, and that's a shame. All the best magic tricks are done close up. That's part of the—"

She was interrupted when a small girl in the front row sneezed. Adriana reached into her pocket and handed the little girl a red handkerchief. "Bless you," Adriana said.

"Thank you," the girl answered as Adriana took a step back.

But there was something surprising about the handkerchief, and both the girl and Adriana watched in amazement as a blue handkerchief, tied to the first, came out of Adriana's pocket. Adriana tugged on it, and a yellow one emerged. A green handkerchief followed, then another red one, and another and another, until a small pile of handkerchiefs lay at the girl's feet.

For the next half hour, Adriana maintained a constant patter of jokes and small talk as she did card tricks, pulled rabbits and doves out of her hat, and juggled. She involved several of the children in her act, giving them bunnies to hold, pretending to pull coins and eggs from their ears, letting them choose cards from her deck.

The children were delighted.

For her finale she produced a length of rope from her top hat. "Who will help me?" she asked. Then her eyes settled on Nancy. "Aha! A volunteer!"

She explained that she wanted Nancy to tie her to a chair. "And make certain the knots are tight."

Nancy worked for several minutes, using all her best knots. At last she stepped away. "There," she said. "You'll never get out of that!"

Nancy returned to her seat, and several audience members stepped up to check the knots. The last was Dr. McGill, who said, "If she escapes from this, I'll eat her top hat!"

The magician nodded to a nurse, who wheeled one of the room dividers in front of her so that the audience couldn't see her. For long moments the audience fidgeted.

Then Dr. McGill called, "Ms. Polidori, are you all right?" There was no answer. "Ms. Polidori?" Now the doctor was concerned, and she told the nurse to move the divider aside.

When she did, the audience gasped!

Chapter

Ten

T HERE SAT ADRIANA, reading a newspaper, her limbs totally free of the ropes!

The audience broke out in amazed cries and applause.

Adriana grinned like the Cheshire cat. She took off her hat and extended it to Dr. McGill. "Hungry?" she asked.

Everybody laughed.

"How'd she do that?" Ned whispered.

"You'll just have to ask her," Nancy teased.

After the show, as Adriana mingled with the audience, Nancy, George, and Ned approached her.

"Hello," the magician called to them. "Did you like my performance?"

"It was wonderful," George said sincerely.

"Just how did you manage to get out of Nancy's knots?" Ned asked.

"It's an old Houdini trick," Adriana explained. "The secret is to grab a bit of slack while the knots are being tied. Nancy thought she had tied the bonds tight, but they were really loose from the start. As she tied them, I breathed in, expanding my chest, so that the loop you put around my body slipped when I relaxed. Then I wiggled until I could get my hands on a knot and started untying."

"Now that's the sort of secret you can't find in books," Ned said appreciatively.

Dr. McGill came over then and asked Adriana to sign autographs for the children.

"Would you mind if I came around to their ward in a few minutes?" she asked. "I want to get out this costume."

Then she fixed her deep green eyes on Nancy. "And, I think that Nancy and I need to have a little talk—"

Nancy raised her brows.

When the doctor wandered away, Adriana touched her arm. "There's a little lounge down the hall. Can you spare a few minutes?"

"Of course," she replied, smiling at Ned.

"George and I will meet you in the front waiting area," he said smoothly.

Nancy nodded, then followed Adriana to an exit at the far end of the cafeteria. When they reached the lounge, Adriana gestured for her to sit down, then collapsed onto the sofa across from her.

"Whew," she said, taking a handkerchief out of her pocket and running it across her brow. "It was hot in there."

Despite the magician's air of casualness, all of Nancy's sense were on alert. Of course, she'd wanted to talk to her, but somehow she hadn't expected Adriana to take the lead.

Adriana twisted the handkerchief in her hand. Nancy could tell that she was having a hard time choosing her words. "What a surprise it was to see you at the restaurant last night," she finally said.

Nancy smiled. "Yes, it was."

"Your father is a wonderful man," she went on quietly. "I've never met anyone quite like him."

Nancy's expression softened. "He *is* wonderful. I'm very lucky to have him for a dad."

Then Adriana frowned. "This morning I had breakfast with another man," she began. "Misha."

The two of them remained silent for a moment.

"To be honest," Nancy said, "I was wondering about that. You know, he threatened me in the parking lot at Riverfront yesterday. He really wants you to leave Conklin Falls."

Adriana sighed deeply. "Please forgive him.

He has a volatile nature. And he's quite . . . attached to me."

"So I gathered," Nancy commented dryly. She crossed her legs and put her hands on one thigh. "I really don't mean to pry," she went on carefully, "but I need to know about the two of you— for the sake of the case."

Adriana shrugged. "What can I say? Misha loves me. He's asked me to marry him more than once." The magician began removing bobby pins from her hair and shaking it loose. "But to me, he is a dear friend, nothing more. Unfortunately, he won't take no for an answer, and he is very possessive sometimes."

Relief flooded through Nancy. She was overjoyed to learn that Adriana wasn't really involved with Grigov. But she kept her face impassive. "Can you imagine him feeling so strongly about getting you away from Riverfront that he'd sabotage the place?"

"Oh," Adriana half-cried out, shaking her head energetically, "absolutely not! He'd never do anything like that! First of all because he'd never hurt me, and second, because it would be illegal."

"But, Adriana," Nancy said, "yesterday around six a man driving a black sports car very much like his just about ran me over the cliff on River Bluff Road. It was definitely intentional."

The magician gasped. "Thank heaven you're all right. But it couldn't have been Misha! He was with me at about that time, I think—and this morning he told me about something strange that happened to him last night—" She looked at Nancy. "Only now, it doesn't seem so strange."

"What?" Nancy asked.

"When he left his room at the motel to go for his supper, his car wasn't in the lot where he'd left it," Adriana explained.

Nancy's eyes widened with astonishment.

"He got very upset, as you can imagine, went to the police, and filed a report," she went on a little breathlessly. "But when he got back to the motel later, the car was there!"

"Amazing," Nancy said.

However, it did occur to her that the car-theft business could have been an elaborate ploy to give Grigov an alibi. He could have tried to run her off the road around six, then ditched his car and reported it stolen. It would have been easy enough to pick up the car later and let the police know that it had miraculously reappeared.

"So, you see," the magician said happily, as if positive that she'd proven her point, "it couldn't have been Misha who tried to hurt you yesterday."

"Uh-huh," Nancy replied, only half listening to Adriana. She said, "I still want to talk to your friend."

"That's easy enough," the magician replied. "He's staying at the Conklin Falls Motel, just across from the golf course on the north side of town."

"Okay." Nancy focused on Adriana and smiled slightly. "And thank you for being so open with me. It was a great help."

After her talk with Adriana, Nancy met Ned and George again. They decided to get some lunch before launching into the day's investigations and stopped at a deli. The guy who made their sandwiches told them about a small park where they could eat.

They found the park easily. While they ate, Nancy told George and Ned everything that Adriana had said.

"Do you believe her?" Ned asked.

"Frankly, I do—or else she's the best liar I ever ran into." She took a bite of her pastrami hero. "It's Grigov I doubt," she said, then went on to explain her theory about how the knife thrower could have staged the disappearance of his car. "I wonder if Sheriff Pulaski ever questioned him."

"You'd think he would have, since Grigov must have run into Pulaski when he reported that his car had been stolen," George speculated.

Nancy gave her friend a skeptical look. "I wouldn't count on it. The sheriff treated us like we were crazy yesterday. I can just imagine the way Grigov could have snowed him."

"Right," George replied. "So now the sheriff's searching for a car thief instead of a saboteur."

"Anyway, I want to talk to Grigov myself," Nancy said.

"And track down Benny Gotnick," George added.

"And have a chat with that realtor," Ned said. A few minutes later he checked his watch. "It's close to two," he said, taking their garbage to a bin. "I don't know how you're going to do it all."

"It's not going to be easy," Nancy replied.

"Look," Ned said, "I've got a racquetball date with my dad at four. But why don't I stop in at Matthews Realty on my way back to Mapleton? If I get a lead on who Matthews's secret client is, I'll leave a message on your machine at home."

Nancy grinned at him. "That sounds great. I really appreciate it. That means George and I can head straight over to Gotnick's."

Half an hour later George and Nancy pulled up in front of Benny Gotnick's run-down house. "Here we are," Nancy said, shutting off the car engine. "He's probably at work, which means that I should be able to check out the inside."

Nancy and George got out of the car and walked through the weeds toward the side of the ramshackle house. Through a window, Nancy peered inside.

She gasped at what she saw.

George joined her at the window.

Amid the threadbare furnishings, a man lay on the floor, facedown in a pool of blood. A large knife was embedded in his back. The knife had a pearl handle, just like the one that belonged to Mikhail Grigov.

Chapter

Eleven

B ENNY GOTNICK," George guessed.

"Worse than that, George," Nancy said, falling back against the house, "he's got Mikhail Grigov's knife in his back."

George let out a low whistle. "Grigov's in real trouble now."

"You bet he is." Nancy shook her head, trying to erase the image of Benny Gotnick from her eyes. "We'd better call Pulaski. I don't want him complaining that we disturbed a crime scene."

Nancy and George got back in the Mustang and drove until they found a pay phone. They reached the sheriff and reported the information about Gotnick. The sheriff told her he'd be over right away, and Nancy hung up the phone.

"There's just one thing I don't get," George

said as she and Nancy headed back to Gotnick's place.

"What's that?" Nancy asked.

George pursed her lips and thought for a moment. "Why would Grigov want to kill Benny? If Gotnick really was the saboteur, there wouldn't be any reason for Grigov to want him dead. It doesn't make sense."

Nancy pulled to a stop in front of Gotnick's house. "You're right, George. But with Grigov's temper, it's hard to be sure. Maybe they were accomplices, and they had a falling out. Who knows? When Pulaski gets here, we can find out what he made of the car theft thing yesterday. Also we can't be sure Grigov did this until the lab checks the knife for fingerprints."

Within minutes Benny Gotnick's house was swarming with police. An ambulance arrived, then a van from the coroner's office. Sheriff Pulaski was among the first on the scene. He spent a few moments directing his deputies, then called Nancy and George over to talk.

After hearing how they had discovered the body, as well as Nancy's suspicions about who the knife belonged to, the sheriff said, "Well, the victim still had his wallet, and his license confirms that he's Gotnick. What do you know about this guy?"

"Virtually nothing, except that he used to work at Riverfront Park and had some gambling debts," Nancy answered.

"Not a bad start," the sheriff said. "The question is—how did he know Grigov?"

"That's what we were wondering," Nancy countered. "We heard all about his stolen car," Nancy went on.

"Yes," Pulaski replied, running a hand through his graying hair. He looked decidedly chagrined. "When the squad car brought him into the station to file a report, I talked to him. What can I say? I believed him."

"And you didn't believe us," George suggested.

The sheriff shook his head. "It wasn't that, exactly. I just figured that whoever stole the car was the one who cut too close to you on River Bluff. I never suspected Grigov. I had no reason to," he insisted.

Nancy smiled slightly.

"Of course, I thought it was strange when his car turned up back in the parking lot later that night. But you know, there are kids who like to 'borrow' cool-looking cars and go for joy rides."

Nancy knew that what he said was true. Still, there was no way the sheriff could keep doubting her about Grigov now.

Nancy glanced back into Benny's living room. To her trained eyes, the Conklin Falls Police Department seemed to be doing an adequate job of sealing off the area and taking photographs. But so far her confidence in their abilities wasn't running high. She decided to do a little investigating herself, just in case they missed something in Gotnick's apartment. Fortunately, Sheriff Pulaski had no objections.

By now the coroner had removed the body, and there was a grisly chalk outline of the spot where Benny had fallen. Nancy stepped around the marks, her eyes searching the room for clues.

The living room was a jumble of magazines, newspapers, and books, and there was trash everywhere.

"Benny Gotnick sure wasn't very neat," George said, surveying the mess.

"It's going to make it hard to find clues," said Nancy. "Look for scraps of paper with phone numbers on them. That sort of thing. Just don't disturb anything."

"I'll try not to," said George. "But who'd know anyway?"

While George searched the living room, Nancy went into the bedroom. Chaos reigned there, too. Drawers were open, with clothes spilling out of them. The closet door was ajar, and Nancy gingerly tugged it open the rest of the way with a pencil she dug out of her purse.

On the floor of Gotnick's closet, half covered by an old T-shirt, Nancy spotted something metallic. She bent over and looked at it closely. It was a large, greasy pin, about the diameter of a knitting needle.

"Bingo!" she cried.

"Find something?" George asked, appearing at the door to the bedroom.

"Get Pulaski," Nancy urged.

A few moments later the sheriff came into the room along with one of his men. Nancy pointed to the floor of the closet. "That's the missing evidence from the roller coaster ride," she told them. "It's the cotter pin that connected the wheel block to the bottom of the car. It proves that the Typhoon accident was rigged."

Pulaski turned to his officer. "Get the photographer in here," he said.

"Good work, Nan," said George. "Now we know Gotnick was involved in the sabotage."

"It sure appears that way," Pulaski agreed. "Thanks for your help, Nancy. I've already sent a man out to Grigov's motel to bring him in for questioning. I'll let you know what develops."

"What next, Nan?" George asked as they got into the Mustang several minutes later.

Nancy checked her watch, then started the car. "It's close to five. The police will take care of Grigov for the moment. Right now I want to talk to my father about how Gotnick's death and the fact that I found the missing pin from the ride affect the case. Remember, the hearing about closing the park is tomorrow morning."

"Right," George replied.

"I'll drop you off at home on my way to my dad's office," Nancy said.

During the drive down the parkway, Nancy mulled over the latest turn of events. George was right—if Gotnick was behind the sabotage, it didn't make sense for Grigov to want him dead. But that would be true of anyone who might have teamed up with Gotnick to sabotage the park— like Vince Garraty and Freda Clarke and whoever had put in the bid to buy Riverfront.

Nancy wondered whether Ned had had any success with the realtor, Larry Matthews. She definitely wanted to know who the secret buyer was.

The scenery passed by in a blur as Nancy tried to come up with a theory that might make all the pieces of the puzzle fit together. She had no success.

By now Nancy was pulling into George's driveway. She stopped the car and gave her friend a quick hug. "You're the best, George Fayne. Thanks for coming along. I'll give you a call when I get home."

She smiled fondly as she watched George clump up the walk in her cast, then put the car in gear and pulled out.

It was almost six by the time she reached Carson Drew's office. Most of the nine-to-fivers had cleared out, and the area around Courthouse Square was deserted as was the lobby of her father's building.

Nancy dashed into the elevator and hit the button for her father's floor. When she got off, she found the large glass door to the office closed and the lights off. She felt fairly certain that she'd find her father still there, because he often worked late. She reached into her purse for the magnetic card he had given her to open the front door.

She unlocked it and strode purposefully across the reception area, then down the hall to her father's office. His door was half open, and she saw light coming from inside. Without breaking stride, Nancy pushed open the door, calling out, "Hey, Dad."

One peek inside made Nancy freeze in her tracks. Carson Drew was there, but so was Adriana Polidori.

The two of them were standing in front of his large window, locked in an embrace!

Chapter

Twelve

CARSON AND ADRIANA gaped at Nancy.

Then the beautiful magician edged herself out of Carson's arms, and Nancy's father stepped back.

Nancy's gaze ricocheted between them. She felt her face flush with embarrassment.

"Nancy—" her father began.

"It isn't what you think—" Adriana explained at the same time.

Suddenly Nancy laughed, and they both stopped. Nancy couldn't help herself. Somehow she felt like a parent, and that was ridiculous. *They* were the adults. Besides, she liked Adriana —especially now that she knew she wasn't involved with Grigov.

She grinned at them. "Will you two stop acting like kids?" she said with a twinkle.

An expression of relief passed across her father's face.

Adriana regained her poise and stepped toward her. "It really wasn't what you're thinking," she said, touching Nancy on the arm. "You see, Misha called me from the Conklin Falls Police Station and told me he'd been arrested on suspicion of murdering Benny Gotnick. I was extremely upset and rushed right here to talk to your father." She glanced back at Carson. "He was only comforting me."

Nancy noticed that Adriana held a crumpled tissue in her hand.

"Grigov is a very old friend of Adriana's," Carson added.

"*Friend* is right, but I know he couldn't have killed Gotnick. I simply can't sit by and see him put in jail for something he couldn't do. It would be all my fault."

"So let's sit down and discuss this calmly," Carson said, suddenly all business. "I need to know everything you discovered at Gotnick's, Nancy, because I'm going to be defending Grigov at his bail hearing tomorrow afternoon."

"But isn't the hearing about the park scheduled for tomorrow, too?" Nancy asked.

"You bet," said Carson. He shot Nancy a wry grin. "But we Drews do pretty well under pressure, don't we?"

Nancy sat in one of the chairs facing her father's desk, and Adriana sank into the other.

Nancy proceeded to tell them the whole story about finding Gotnick. When she got to the part about the cotter pin, Carson's eyes widened in amazement.

"That proves the ride was sabotaged. It will be very important tomorrow—and vital information for the state inspectors next week. Good work, Nancy!" he said.

"I'm almost sure that it was Grigov's knife I saw in Gotnick's back," Nancy continued.

Adriana winced.

"Pulaski must have prints," Carson said, "or else he couldn't hold Grigov."

"This is bad, isn't it?" Adriana asked.

Torn, Nancy tried to reassure the magician. "It's all still circumstantial," she said. Privately she had her doubts about Grigov, but she was trying to keep an open mind. After all, the man was innocent until she could prove him guilty.

Adriana sighed deeply. "Maybe I should just sell the park. Someone doesn't want me to keep it open." She dabbed the corners of her eyes with a tissue. "If only we knew who Matthews's client is."

"What's happening on that angle?" Carson asked Nancy.

"Ned went to see the realtor this afternoon," Nancy told her father. "That reminds me, I want to check the machine at home to see if he left a message about what he discovered."

"You can use the phone on my secretary's desk," her father offered.

"Great," Nancy said, heading out of the office. She called her home number and entered the message playback code. There was a beep, then Ned's voice:

"Hi, Nan, it's Ned. Boy, do I have some news for you! I stopped by Matthews Realty. The boss was gone, so I chatted up his secretary—don't worry, she's not half as gorgeous as you. Anyway, she wouldn't reveal who Larry Matthews's client is, but she did say that Riverfront is a valuable piece of property, provided the buyer can get it zoned to suit his purposes."

There was a pause, then Ned's voice started up again: "I hope this tape doesn't run out, because there's more. I started thinking about the zoning thing after I left Matthews's. So, on a hunch, I went over to the Conklin Falls Hall of Records. And I found some pretty interesting stuff there.

"It turns out that back during Prohibition some old-time gangster dug a million tunnels under Riverfront for storage. In fact, the system is so extensive that the city considers the land on top of them unstable and won't rezone the property for development of any kind. But there's a legal loophole. The amusement park was built back when zoning regulations were less strict. It can stay there forever. It just can't be replaced—by anything. Pretty amazing, huh?

"I'm going straight back to Matthews's now to tell him what I found out. In exchange for the information, I figure he'll open up about who his client is. I'll call you from home with the news."

Nancy put her finger on the receiver button, waited for the dial tone, and then dialed Ned's home number. His mother answered.

"Hi, Mrs. Nickerson. It's Nancy. Is Ned home yet?"

"Nancy," she said, "I'm so relieved you called. Ned's not home. In fact, he didn't show up for his racquetball date with his father, and I'm worried about him."

Nancy frowned. "He was doing some legwork for a case I'm on. Maybe he got tied up," she said.

"But it's not like Ned not to call," Mrs. Nickerson protested.

Nancy had to agree, but she told Ned's mom to stay calm. Still, she felt a twinge of concern when she hung up.

Back in her father's office, Nancy filled Adriana and Carson in on what Ned had learned.

"Tunnels beneath the park!" the magician exclaimed. "Uncle Nicos never said anything about them. I wonder if he even knew."

"It's strange that someone would want to buy the park if the city of Conklin Falls won't zone the land for rebuilding," Nancy said, trying to remember the details of Ned's message.

"You'd think a potential buyer would know about that," Carson put in, "or at least his realtor would."

"Could the buyer want something that's hidden in the tunnels?" Adriana wondered aloud.

"It's a possibility," Nancy agreed. "But I don't know why the person couldn't just sneak down there and look."

"Making an offer to purchase the park *is* going to a lot of trouble," Carson said.

"Look, Dad," Nancy said, "I can't sit still until I get to the bottom of this. I'm going back up to Conklin Falls to see if I can catch Larry Matthews. He may still be around."

"Why not wait for Ned to call back?" her father asked.

"I don't know where he is," she explained, anxiety tightening her voice.

Carson frowned. "Just be careful. This case is getting pretty ugly."

"I know," Nancy agreed.

"I'll try not to be home too late," he went on. "But if you're in bed by the time I get there, remember we have to be at the courthouse at nine-thirty tomorrow morning."

Nancy said goodbye. As she was leaving the office, she took a last glance over her shoulder at Carson and Adriana. Their heads were bent over the desk together conspiratorially. Nancy made a silent wish that her father wasn't setting himself up for disappointment as far as Adriana Polidori was concerned.

All the way back to Conklin Falls, Nancy's mind was on Ned. It was strange that no one had heard from him since late that afternoon. She kept trying to think through his steps. He'd gone to Matthews's office, the Hall of Records, back to the realtor's—and then? Had he learned something important from Matthews? And could it have gotten him into trouble?

On the other hand, maybe he ran into a friend. Maybe they went out and lost track of time. Maybe that was why he didn't call his dad to tell him he couldn't make it to the racquetball court.

Before Nancy had left her father's office she'd looked up Matthews Realty in the telephone book and written down the address. The office was in downtown Conklin Falls. Nancy drove as if her life depended on it, arriving at the realtor's twenty minutes later. She pulled to a stop in front just as the sky was turning dark.

She climbed the three steps to the building, tried the glass door, and found it locked. After knocking for several minutes, Nancy spotted a light as it was clicked on and saw a woman approach the door.

"We're closed," she called without opening up. She was dressed in a tailored blue business suit, and her platinum blond hair fell around her heart-shaped face in a flattering style. Nancy guessed she was the secretary Ned had spoken with. The woman started walking away.

"Please!" Nancy shouted. "You've got to help. I'm in trouble, and I need to talk to you."

Now the secretary stopped in her tracks and turned back. "What do you want?" she asked suspiciously.

"My boyfriend's in trouble," Nancy said, desperation straining her voice. "Please. I think you met him earlier today."

The woman stared at Nancy for several long moments. Finally she opened the door for her. "Are you talking about the guy who wanted to know who's trying to buy Riverfront?" she asked. Her eyes narrowed as she waited for Nancy to reply.

"Can I come in?" Nancy pleaded. Without waiting for an answer, she stepped past the woman and into the office.

Inside, the walls of the realty office were lined with photographs of old Conklin Falls buildings. Behind the reception area were five desks, all covered with big binders and stacks of paper. A computer terminal stood in one corner along with a fax machine.

"What kind of trouble is your boyfriend in?" the woman asked.

"I need to know if you saw him later on today. Did he come back?" Nancy pressed.

The woman seemed to be really confused now. "Yes, he did," she said at last. "But by then Mr.

Matthews was in. So your boyfriend met with him."

Nancy took a deep breath. "I think something's happened to him because of what he learned from your boss. You have to tell me who's trying to buy Riverfront Park!"

The secretary shook her head firmly. "No way. That's confidential information. And I don't see what it could have to do with your boyfriend."

Nancy was losing her patience. "Then let me call Mr. Matthews."

"He went out of town late this afternoon," she replied. "He's driving to Harper's Grove to check out some property. You'll have to come back tomorrow."

"I can't wait until tomorrow," Nancy insisted.

"Look, I shouldn't even be talking to you." She strode to the door and held it open for Nancy. "Please leave."

With a sigh, Nancy realized she wasn't going to get any further with the woman. She gave her a final imploring look, then glanced around the office. If only there was a way to search the place. Suddenly she thought of something.

"Can I use the bathroom before I go?" Nancy asked, biting her lip.

The secretary sighed irritably. "It's in the hall. I'll show you."

Out in the hallway, she pointed to a door marked Ladies.

"I'll wait for you here," she said.

Nancy let herself into the bathroom and nearly shouted with joy when she saw that she was in luck. The bathroom had a window, which Nancy was able to open. She only hoped that the woman wouldn't check the ladies' room when she locked up the office.

"Thanks," said Nancy, emerging from the ladies' room.

"You'd better leave now," she replied curtly.

Nancy allowed the woman to show her out. She started up her car and drove off. After turning onto the next block, Nancy pulled into an alley and shut off her car.

She waited for twenty minutes, then drove back to Matthews's office. The lights were out, and there were no cars out front. She drove into an alley beside the building and made her way to the window she'd left open. It was still ajar.

"All right!" Nancy cried, heaving herself up and inside.

The hallway outside Matthews's office was dark, and Nancy was careful to stay in the shadows. Naturally, the door to the office was locked. Nancy checked around the jamb for any alarm wires and found none. Then she pulled her lockpick out of her purse. Within minutes she had the door open and was inside!

At the back of the office stood a partition. Nancy guessed that Matthews's desk was behind it. She crossed the room quietly, keeping low and out of sight.

The man's desk was a jumble of papers, binders, books, and computer printouts. Nancy found her flashlight in her shoulder bag and quickly scanned the papers, searching for any kind of document that had Riverfront's name on it.

Ten minutes later she'd gone through everything on the desk and in Matthews's drawers. None of the folders in the file cabinets had anything to do with Riverfront.

"He probably took them with him," Nancy said aloud. "Rats!"

On a hunch, Nancy searched through the garbage pail underneath the desk. Among the trash, she found a pink message slip that had been wadded up. She smoothed it out and her jaw dropped in surprise as she read what was written on it.

It was a record of a call for Larry Matthews from Vince Garraty. Beneath Garraty's name and number was a scrawled message:

"Call him ASAP about his offer on Riverfront Park."

Chapter

Thirteen

THE MYSTERIOUS BUYER for Riverfront Park was Vince Garraty!

What did it mean? Was this just his way of helping out his fiancée? But then why had Benny Gotnick been killed? Benny Gotnick worked for Vince. What did that have to do with it?

Nancy read the message again, but it didn't answer her questions. Her mind still spinning, she tucked it into her bag, switched off her flashlight, and tiptoed back through the office.

She exited by the bathroom window, pushing it shut after her.

All the way back to River Heights, Nancy pondered the possibilities. Garraty and Gotnick. It made sense. Garraty wanted the park—maybe because of Freda or maybe for some other reason. When Benny got fired, the two of them teamed up, with Benny rigging the flaming carpet and the Typhoon derailment. The more accidents the better as far as Garraty was concerned. Bad press would convince Adriana to sell, and it would drive down the price of the property.

Then maybe Benny got cold feet, and Garraty killed him. It could have been Garraty who stole Grigov's car and tried to run her off the road. He could have gotten Grigov's knife out of the trunk of the car.

For a minute she considered turning around and heading back to the Conklin Falls Police Department to talk to Sheriff Pulaski. She had no proof of Garraty's involvement, though—only a little piece of paper that suggested he wanted to buy the park.

It was past eight by the time she pulled into her driveway. The house was dark, which meant her father still wasn't home. Nancy threw her jacket on the coatrack and went straight for the phone.

The light on the answering machine was blinking, but when she played the tape back, all she heard was Ned's long message from that afternoon. She erased it, reset the machine, then dialed his number. The line was busy, so she called George instead.

Her friend was amazed to hear all that had happened. "I never liked Garraty," she said, then paused. "But, you know, I'm more concerned about Ned."

"Same here," Nancy answered, her stomach

twisting with apprehension. "I'm going to keep trying his house until I get through. I just hope he's sitting in front of the tube." But she didn't believe her own words.

She told George she'd call her right away if she heard anything, then arranged to pick her up the next morning for the hearing.

Next, she called Ned back. This time his mother answered.

"Oh, Nancy," she cried, "Ned still hasn't come home. He hasn't called either. We've contacted all the area hospitals, but no one has a record of his being in an accident. His father and I are out of our minds with worry!"

Nancy tried to stay calm. "Did you call the police, too?"

"We just did," Mrs. Nickerson told her. "But they said we have to wait twenty-four hours before filing a missing person report. . . ." Her voice trailed off, and Nancy knew she was crying.

Then Mr. Nickerson took the phone. "Nancy, what do you know about this?" he asked.

"Ned was helping me on a case," she explained a little weakly. "He went to a realtor's office in Conklin Falls this afternoon, then to the Hall of Records. I haven't heard from him since."

Mr. Nickerson remained silent.

"Can I come over there?" Nancy offered. "Maybe it would help—"

"Thanks, Nancy," he said, then paused again, "but that's not necessary. I know there's a good explanation for this. I don't think we should panic."

"Will you call me the minute you hear anything?" Nancy asked.

"Absolutely," he replied.

Nancy said goodbye and hung up, a feeling of dread washing over her. But there was nothing she could do except wait.

She stared with unfocused eyes for a moment, then opened her shoulder bag and took out her wallet. It contained a picture of Ned inside a clear plastic holder. For a long moment she gazed at the face she loved so much. If anything had happened to him, she would never forgive herself.

"So you think Garraty and Gotnick were behind the sabotage?" George said.

It was early the next morning. Nancy had spent a fitful night worrying about Ned. She'd called the Nickersons right after she woke up, but they still hadn't heard anything. She decided there was nothing she could do to find Ned right then, so she and George headed to Conklin Falls for the hearing. She believed Ned could take care of himself in almost any situation. Carson had gone on ahead to prepare Adriana.

"I'm not positive," Nancy told her friend, "but it seems likely. As soon as this hearing's over, I plan to find Garraty. The man has a few questions to answer."

"You don't think Garraty has anything to do with Ned's disappearance, do you?" George wondered aloud.

Nancy took the Conklin Falls exit off the parkway and stopped at a red light. "If Ned got Garraty's name out of Matthews and went after the guy, there's a chance Garraty was the last one to see him before he disappeared." The light turned green, and Nancy pulled into the line of cars headed for town.

The sun was coming out from behind a cloud as Nancy drove into the parking lot of the Conklin Falls courthouse. Already there was a lot of activity, with attorneys and their clients coming in and going out of the three-story brick building. Nancy found a parking spot, and the two friends made their way to the courtroom where Carson would be defending Adriana at her hearing.

Inside, Nancy quickly spotted Freda Clarke sitting with her son and her lawyer. Carson and Adriana occupied a table across the aisle from them. George and Nancy hurried over and sat behind them.

"Hello there," Carson said to Nancy, turning in his seat.

Adriana turned, too. She wore a dark green suit and had her hair pulled back into a chignon —she looked devastating as usual. "Thank you for coming," she whispered. "I can use the moral support."

Carson had gotten in late the night before, and Nancy hadn't had the chance to tell him about Ned or her latest lead. "Dad—" she said, leaning forward in her seat.

"Not now, Nancy," Carson said. He gestured toward the bench, where the judge had just sat down. "We're about to start."

"I hope this doesn't take long," Nancy said. To their right, Freda Clarke and her lawyer were conferring. Chris spotted George and gave her a wave.

"You're thinking about Ned, aren't you?" George said.

Nancy nodded and frowned slightly. "The longer we wait, the more worried I get."

"Hmmm," George said, her eyes focused toward the aisle behind Nancy, "I wonder what he's doing here?"

"Who?" Nancy asked.

"Rand Hagan just walked in," George answered.

Nancy swung around. George was right. The Riverfront engineer was heading into the courtroom. He was dressed in jeans and a leather jacket and had his trademark bandanna tied around his neck.

When he paused in the aisle between them and Freda Clarke, Adriana caught sight of him, too.

She looked surprised. "Rand," she said, "what are you doing here?"

Hagan smiled and wrinkles appeared at the

corners of his blue eyes. "I'm going to testify. Why else would I be here?"

Nancy watched Adriana stand up, a smile on her face. She stepped across the aisle toward Hagan and said, "That's very kind of you."

"You'd better wait before you thank me," Hagan said.

"I don't understand." Adriana blinked in confusion.

Nancy saw Hagan's smile turn nasty. "I'm not here to testify for *you,* Adriana. I'm here to help Freda Clarke. I'm going to tell the judge what a dangerous, badly maintained place Riverfront Park is."

Chapter

Fourteen

I CAN'T BELIEVE IT!" George gasped. "He seemed like such a nice guy."

Nancy watched Adriana first recoil from Hagan then sink back into her chair. Carson put his arm around her. "It's okay," he said, trying to reassure her.

Rand pointed his finger at Adriana and said, "Your uncle couldn't manage the place, and neither can you. That's what I'm prepared to state today. Riverfront needs to be in the hands of someone who knows and understands the meaning of the word *safety!*"

Freda Clarke's eyes went wide, obviously as surprised as Adriana to see a new witness come forward. She glanced at Nancy and smiled smugly, then went back to conferring with her attorney.

"Dad," Nancy said, leaning forward, "he can't just show up and testify, can he?"

Carson spoke over his shoulder. "I'm afraid he can, Nancy. This is a public hearing, and anyone can come forward to speak."

The judge called the hearing to order. For the next two hours Nancy squirmed as first Freda and then Hagan told their stories. Hagan reported that things had been lax at the park under Nicos Polidori, but that when Adriana came on, matters grew worse. She cut corners in an effort to save money. He said he'd tried to persuade her to upgrade the rides because they weren't safe, but she wouldn't do it.

Hagan's words had the ring of expertise. He was a compelling and credible witness. The judge's expression was solemn as he listened to Hagan's testimony, and Adriana paled.

Even under Carson Drew's strenuous cross-examination, neither witness broke down. When Carson put Adriana on the stand, Nancy was riveted as the woman told a moving story about her uncle Nicos and how he'd worked his whole life to make the park what it was. Then Adriana described her plans for the place while the judge listened intently.

Carson finished up by explaining that new evidence had been discovered indicating that the Typhoon had been sabotaged. He mentioned the cotter pin found at the scene of Benny Gotnick's murder.

In the end the judge ruled against allowing Riverfront to remain open until the state inspectors arrived the following week. "They'll make a final determination about what caused the roller coaster derailment," he said. "Until then, there are too many unanswered questions about the safety of the park. I'd be irresponsible if I allowed Riverfront to remain open. Children's lives are at stake."

With that the judge banged his gavel and called the hearing to an end.

"That's it?" Nancy wondered aloud.

Carson was putting away his papers. "I'm afraid so," he said. Then he turned to Adriana, "I'm sorry, but Rand Hagan's testimony did us in."

Adriana nodded sadly.

Just then Nancy noticed Freda and Chris Clarke making their way out of the courtroom. Freda stopped as she passed Rand Hagan and shook his hand. Rand gave her a smile and then walked out with her.

Nancy stood up abruptly, giving her father and Adriana a quick goodbye. "Come on, George." She grabbed her friend's arm.

"Where are we going?" George wanted to know, hobbling behind Nancy.

"We're following Hagan," Nancy said.

"Right," George replied, not skipping a beat.

"Then we're going to find Ned," Nancy added. "I've waited long enough."

Out in the parking lot, Rand Hagan was getting into a beat-up pickup truck. Nancy and George rushed over to her Mustang and pulled out just behind Hagan.

"Don't get too close," George warned her as they cruised to a stop right behind Hagan.

"Don't worry," Nancy said. The light turned green, and after going through it, Nancy allowed another car to come between hers and Hagan's. "I'm a pro at this, remember?"

"How could I forget?" George asked.

Hagan led them on a tour of downtown Conklin Falls. Nancy and George waited while Rand went to the bank, picked up his dry cleaning, and stopped by a video store. After the last errand, though, Hagan got on the main road out of town, headed toward Riverfront.

"He's making for the park," George guessed.

"It looks that way," Nancy agreed. Since there was little traffic, she hung back, just keeping Hagan's pickup in sight.

"There's one thing I don't get," George said. "What made Hagan betray Adriana? Didn't you say she trusted him completely? And he seemed like such a nice man! He even rescued us!"

"I know," Nancy replied. "The only thing I can think is that Vince Garraty got to him and convinced him to testify against Adriana. Garraty wants to buy Riverfront. If the place is closed down and gets a lot of bad press, Adriana's more likely to sell out—for a song."

George let out a deep breath. "I see what you mean," she commented. "But why would Garraty want to buy the property if it can't be rezoned. What's he going to do with it?"

Nancy frowned. "I don't know. But I keep thinking about those tunnels."

"That's so weird," George went on. "Who'd ever have thought there were underground passages beneath Riverfront?"

Nancy nodded. They were pulling into the park entrance now. Clouds had covered the sun, and it looked as if it was about to rain. Hagan's pickup was in the parking lot, but Rand had disappeared by the time Nancy steered her Mustang into a spot.

"Nancy, look!" George pointed to a corner of the parking lot. "Isn't that Ned's car?"

Nancy saw Ned's familiar sedan. "But why—" She tried to make sense of what could have happened.

"Do you think he came up here after he talked to Matthews and got into trouble?" George asked.

"There's only one way to find out," Nancy said. "And that's to find Rand Hagan!"

Nancy marched toward the park's main gate. It was locked, but she quickly scaled the chain-link fence, then helped George with her clunky cast. When they got to the other side, George took hold of Nancy's arm.

"We should be careful," she warned. "Hagan could be dangerous."

Nancy nodded in agreement. "You stay here. Keep out of sight. If I'm not back in half an hour, call Pulaski. I hate splitting up like this, but it's the only way to make sure he doesn't nab us both."

"Okay," George agreed. She planted herself beside the ticket booth and checked her watch. "I'll wait right here. Good luck, Nan."

Nancy gave George a hug, then went off down the midway. She kept low and out of sight. She wanted to spot Hagan before he caught sight of her.

There was no sign of Rand at any of the booths or by the merry-go-round. She veered off the midway to the roller coaster, but it was quiet, empty, and rather forlorn. The Whirl-o-Looper was still, too, and so was the tea-cup ride. Nancy was about to give up on finding Rand, when she noticed that the entrance to the Tunnel of Love was open.

"That's strange," she said to herself, heading for the door.

Adriana hadn't gotten around to reopening the Tunnel of Love, but Nancy remembered the ride from when she had come to the park as a kid. It was shaped like a big volcano with a moat encircling it. Inside, a train of cars took riders through decorated rooms. Nancy remembered one that looked like an underwater grotto, complete with a mermaid and sea monster.

Now, as she stepped inside, Nancy saw that the ride had fallen into disrepair. There were cobwebs everywhere. The cars were standing by the front entrance. They looked as if they hadn't been used in years.

Nancy made her way into the Tunnel of Love carefully, trying to keep the soles of her shoes from making any sound on the floor. It was cold and dank in the passageway, and Nancy pulled her jacket closed. Just as she rounded a bend, Nancy spotted a beam of light up ahead.

Hagan, she thought, identifying the man and hugging the wall so he couldn't see her.

The light moved off again. Slowly she crept forward, keeping Hagan in sight.

What's he doing here? she wondered.

Suddenly a rectangular patch of light appeared in the darkness, and Nancy realized that Hagan had opened a door leading off the tunnel. Once the door was closed again, Nancy made her way to the spot. She counted to thirty, giving Hagan time to get ahead of her, then she opened the door.

What Nancy found surprised her. Near her head was a dim lightbulb revealing a rickety flight of steps, leading into the darkness below.

"The bootleggers' tunnels!" she murmured. Obviously, Hagan knew about them. Could it be that they were why Vince Garraty wanted to buy the place? Maybe Hagan had been in on some kind of a plot with Garraty all along . . .

Could this be where Ned was? What if Ned had come here to search and had been caught by Rand?

Nancy had to find out. She stepped carefully onto the steps and slowly descended. When she reached the bottom, she started walking into the gently sloping tunnel. Searching through her shoulder bag, Nancy found her flashlight. Careful to keep the beam low, she made her way deeper into the tunnel's dark cavity.

She walked for a long time and began to despair of finding Hagan. Maybe he hadn't come this way at all.

Then, in the distance, Nancy spotted a dull glow farther down the tunnel. She made her way toward it, hugging the side of the tunnel to keep out of sight.

When she finally came to the end of the passageway, Nancy was shocked to see that the tunnel opened into an enormous chamber as large as a warehouse. Light fixtures strung along its ceiling glowed eerily. Several other passageways led off from the chamber at various points along its walls. Most were narrow, like the one Nancy had traversed, but one was big enough to drive a large truck through.

Rand Hagan stood with his back to her in the middle of the chamber, surrounded by fifty-gallon drums. Each drum had a familiar crosshatched symbol stenciled on it. Nancy's jaw dropped open when she realized what they held —hazardous waste!

The sound of an engine startled her. It was coming from the big tunnel. She pressed herself against the wall just as Hagan turned to wave a truck full of more drums into the chamber. The truck had Garraty's name and slogan painted on its side. Behind the wheel was Vince Garraty himself!

Chapter

Fifteen

VINCE GARRATY WAS DUMPING illegal waste underneath Riverfront Park, Nancy realized. And Rand Hagan was helping him!

"Hagan!" Garraty called out, jumping down from the cab of the truck. "Help me with this stuff!"

While Hagan and Garraty unloaded the truck, Nancy's mind raced. The two men had obviously been working together all along. Hagan must have found out about the tunnels and told Garraty. What better place to dispose of hazardous waste than in underground tunnels?

No wonder Garraty wanted to buy the place, Nancy thought. When Adriana took over the park, he must have figured that he'd be found out—especially when she starting redeveloping

Riverfront as a modern magic theme park. Nancy clicked off her flashlight and leaned into the chamber to get a better view. As she reached out to grasp a rock ledge, her flashlight fell from her hand and clattered to the ground.

"Hey!" Garraty called out. "Who's there?"

"What do you mean?" Hagan demanded.

Nancy saw the two men looking in her direction. She pressed herself against the wall and froze.

"Someone followed you," Garraty said angrily.

"No way," Hagan assured him.

"Just like that kid yesterday never came by," Garraty said.

Ned! Nancy guessed. She watched in horror as Garraty started walking in her direction. She had to get out of there and fast.

How? The only choice was back up the tunnel. In a flash Nancy spun on her heels and took off as fast as she could. She didn't even have time to pick up her flashlight. She'd just have to find her way in the dark.

"I told you there was someone there!" came Garraty's voice. "Get her!"

Her heart racing, Nancy put on speed. She could hear the men's footsteps behind her, gaining fast. She kept running, though all she could see in front of her was a dark hole. If she could just keep going she was sure she could outrun them!

Then she stumbled and fell to her knees. A quick glance behind her told Nancy that Hagan was practically on top of her. She struggled to her feet, but before she could take off running, Hagan grabbed her arm and yanked her toward him hard.

"You!" Hagan said, the beam from his flashlight casting eerie shadows on his face. "You're just too nosy for your own good."

Nancy spun her other arm around and slammed her fist into his stomach. He groaned and dropped to his knees.

Nancy turned and ran for the end of the tunnel, clambering back up the steps. She had just reached the door and was throwing it open when a hand came down on her shoulder.

It was Garraty. He had a fierce gleam in his eyes. "Not so fast, Nancy Drew," he growled.

Then he raised his arm above his head and brought the butt of a gun down on her head. Everything went black.

When Nancy awoke, she realized the tightness at her arms and legs meant she was tied up. At her back, she felt warmth and movement. She still felt dazed but gradually she became aware of someone calling out her name.

She recognized the voice. Twisting around, Nancy saw Ned tied up with his back to her.

"Ned!" Nancy cried with relief. "Are you okay?"

"I should ask you the same thing," he said. His hands were bound just as hers were. "I saw them drag you in here and watched them tie you up. There was nothing I could do."

"It's okay," Nancy murmured. "But I was so worried," she said.

"Me, too, Nan," he replied. "I wasn't sure I'd ever see you again."

"Where are we?" Nancy asked, looking around.

"Don't you recognize the place?" Ned asked. "It's the prop and pyrotechnics room just off the auditorium."

Nancy noticed the long worktables and the flame retardant tank she'd checked out the night they'd seen the show. At the far end of the room was a door marked Danger: Explosives. "Have you been tied up here ever since yesterday?" she asked.

"No," he said. "They locked me in a storeroom in the Tunnel of Love. But they came and got me a few minutes ago and brought me here." He smiled slightly. "You were unconscious when they carried you in, but was I ever glad to see you!"

"But, Ned," she cried, "why did you come to the park yesterday? I got your message about the tunnels and then nothing. Your folks are so worried."

He sighed. "When I left the Hall of Records, I went back to Matthews's, like I said. He wouldn't tell me a thing. But I kept thinking about the tunnels and how important it was for you to know about them. I came to Riverfront, hoping that you might have ended up here. Then I ran into Hagan—and like a fool asked him about the tunnels. He seemed like such a good guy. . . ."

"Oh, he's a great guy," Nancy said, shaking her head in disgust.

"After he tied me up, he told me everything. He sabotaged the ride, Nan, and put kerosene in the tank over there. He's teamed up with Vince Garraty because Garraty wants Riverfront. The two of them have been storing toxic—"

"I know, Ned," she cut in, squirming against the ropes that bound her wrists. "We've got to get out of here," she said. Then she remembered George. More than half an hour had to have passed by now. Her friend was sure to have called the police.

Before Nancy could tell Ned that George was waiting for them, the door flew open and Hagan and Garraty appeared.

"We came to say goodbye," Hagan announced. He knelt down to check Nancy's rope, giving both her and Ned a withering look.

Garraty pried open the door that had the danger sign on it, went inside, and emerged carrying an armload of dynamite. Hanging from his arm was a spool of fuse wire. He handed the dynamite to Hagan, who propped several sticks beside Ned and Nancy.

Nancy watched in horror as Garraty fastened the sticks together with the wire.

"You'll never get away with this," she warned them, trying to keep the desperation out of her voice. "The police are on their way."

"Sorry, but you're wrong," Garraty told her. "The hick cops around here won't be able to figure out what happened, but they'll find two dead kids and that'll be enough to shut this place down forever."

When Garraty was certain that the explosives were secure, he stood back and surveyed his work. "See, here's what the cops are going to think," he explained. "You two broke in, started messing around with stuff you shouldn't have gone near, and accidentally set off a great big explosion. Riverfront Park closes forever, Adriana Polidori sells out to the mystery buyer, no one ever finds out what's in the tunnels."

"End of story," Hagan said with a wicked smile. He ran a length of fuse out toward the door. "What do you think, Vince—is that enough?"

"Yeah, it's great," Garraty answered. Hagan clipped off the fuse with a pocket knife. "This place should go up like rockets on the Fourth of July," he said.

"I just have one question," Nancy said, stalling for time. "Which one of you tried to run me down in Grigov's car?"

"I may as well tell you. That was me," Hagan

put in. "I hot-wired his car and went looking for you. I figured, even if you survived, you'd think it was Grigov who tried to kill you. And then I found the knife in the trunk of his car. Wasn't that convenient?" he asked, his face twisted in an ugly smirk.

"So you killed Benny Gotnick with Grigov's knife," Nancy pressed, "and planted the cotter pin from the roller coaster in his closet."

"Bright girl," Hagan snapped.

Nancy wanted the whole story. She also knew that if she kept the men talking, it wouldn't be long before Pulaski's men would be on their way. All she and Ned had to do was stay alive until someone came looking for them. "How do you two even know each other?" she asked.

Garraty gave her one of his engaging smiles. "We have Benny to thank for that. He introduced us."

"Was he in on this thing, too?" Ned asked.

"For a while," Hagan replied. "Two years ago, Benny and I were working on the Tunnel of Love together, and we found a door we'd never opened before. It led down into these tunnels. Benny saw the possibilities right away. He was up to his eyeballs in debt and figured out a way for all of us to make a ton of money. So he introduced Vince and me."

"I don't get it," Ned interrupted. "How does putting this junk down here make money for you?"

"Simple," Garraty said, taking over the conversation from Hagan. "Let's say a customer wants me to get rid of a hundred barrels of toxic waste. What I used to do was send it to a chemical detox plant in Chicago. But the detox plant charged me an arm and a leg to get rid of every barrel. Are you starting to get my drift?"

"I'm afraid so," Ned answered.

"Dumping the toxic waste in the tunnels is a lot less expensive. It all adds up to big money."

"But those drums could leak into the groundwater and contaminate the river!" she exclaimed.

Garraty just shrugged. "What's it to me?"

"But why all the other crimes?" she asked. "Why kill Benny? Why sabotage the roller coaster and Adriana's act?"

Garraty broke in. "Don't forget to include Nicos," he said, almost smiling.

"Nicos, too?" Ned said incredulously.

"He brought it on himself," Hagan cut in. "He found out what we were doing down here and threatened to call the cops."

"But because we were friends, he gave us the option of just cleaning the wastes out of here," Hagan said. Instead, I left the power on over the midway when it was supposed to be off. He stuck a screwdriver into a socket—and zap, no more Nicos."

"You killed an old friend just like that?" Nancy said, horrified.

"I had to. After the roller coaster derailment, Benny started to get cold feet. He wanted out, so he had to go, too." Hagan explained.

"And Freda Clarke was the perfect tool for you two, wasn't she?" Nancy guessed.

"Absolutely," Garraty said. "Rand and Benny knew all about her lawsuit. It wasn't going anywhere without big money behind it. I called her up, acted interested in her, her lawsuit, even in that bratty kid, and it wasn't long before she was hooked."

Nancy felt terribly sorry for Freda Clarke. "So you don't really care for her at all," she said.

Garraty snickered. "Are you kidding?"

Ned turned his head toward Hagan. "It was nice of you to save me on that ride," he said bitterly. "But why'd you bother?"

Hagan put his hands on his hips and looked at Nancy. "Did you ever suspect that I was the one who'd rigged that accident?"

Nancy stared at him, then replied. "You're right, it was a pretty good move. It was only when you showed up at the hearing that I started to suspect you."

"Enough talk," Garraty warned. He gestured for Hagan to move away. "Sorry, but you two are about to have a tragic accident."

Hagan glanced at Ned and Nancy. "This is a slow-burning fuse, so you've got about two or three minutes to say goodbye to each other. Use it well." He pulled a match from his pocket, lit it, and set fire to the fuse. Then he and Garraty dashed out, slamming the door behind them.

Nancy and Ned stared at the burning fuse in horror. In two minutes it would reach the explosives, and then they would be blown to smithereens!

Chapter

Sixteen

Nancy watched the fuse burn closer and closer to the dynamite.

Behind her, Ned squirmed and strained against his bonds. Nancy felt him inhaling deeply, then heard him letting out the breath.

"What are you doing?" Nancy asked tensely.

"Remember yesterday at the hospital?" Ned replied, gasping as he continued to wiggle around.

"Ned," Nancy burst out, "we've got to do something to get out of here—"

"That's what I *am* doing. Garraty didn't know it, but I tensed up when he tied me up."

Suddenly Nancy realized what he was up to. "You're trying Adriana's trick—the one she got from Houdini. You're amazing. Remind me to give you a big kiss when we get out of this," she said, her voice rising excitedly. "Can you get loose?"

Nancy felt Ned move behind her. "I think it's working!" he yelled.

While Ned worked to free himself, Nancy tried to keep her eyes off the fuse, now burning perilously close to her feet. A wave of panic rolled over her, but she forced herself to keep calm.

"Hurry," she said. "I figure we've only got another minute!"

"I'm out!" Ned announced.

Reaching around to Nancy's back, he dug his fingers into the knot at her wrists. She felt him fumble a little.

"Keep cool," Nancy urged him. "You're doing an incredible job!"

"You're the one who's shouting," Ned said with a grim smile.

He knelt before her now, unfastening her legs. Within another few seconds, Nancy was free!

She sprang to her feet.

Ned glanced toward the dynamite. "How much time do we have?"

"I'm not sticking around to find out!" she cried, running to the door and grabbing the knob. But it was locked!

Together they charged it, crashing into its surface with a bone-crushing thud. It burst outward. They struggled to keep their balance as they careened through, running into the back-stage area and then out the rear door.

Seconds later the back of the building erupted in an enormous, fiery explosion!

The blast picked them up and hurled them yards away. Nancy crashed into a refreshment booth and felt the flimsy wood of the structure splinter under the impact. The wind was knocked out of her, and she lay still for a moment, trying to recover. She felt bruised all over, but nothing seemed to be broken. Then she remembered Ned.

She glanced around and saw him lying on the ground a few yards away. She limped over to him just as he sat up.

"Ned, we made it! Are you okay?" she said, and threw her arms around him.

"Yeah, I think so," he answered, feeling his head with his hands. "But that sure didn't help my concussion!" They laughed and then hugged each other in relief.

Ned looked over at the back of the auditorium, which was in flames. "Before we go after Hagan and Garraty we'd better call the fire department."

"You're right," Nancy said.

Just then, they heard the sound of sirens in the distance. "Someone's already called," Nancy said. She got to her feet and scanned the empty midway. "I wonder what happened to George. I told her to call the police if I didn't come back in half an hour."

"She must have gone off to look for a phone," Ned guessed, then stood up. "Maybe she was the one who called the fire department."

"Well, we don't have time to wait," Nancy said. "Hagan and Garraty will get away if we don't go after them ourselves."

Without another word, she took off running toward the Tunnel of Love, Ned right behind her. The two of them vaulted over the narrow moat that surrounded the ride, and soon they were both pressed up against the outside of the artificial volcano.

"Do you think they've gone back down into the tunnels?" Ned asked.

"Not yet," Nancy guessed. "They'll want to check to see if we're really dead."

They sneaked along the outside of the Tunnel of Love, working their way toward the entrance at the front of the ride. They'd nearly reached it when the door cracked open, and Nancy saw Garraty poking his head out. He peered toward the back of the auditorium, where Nancy and Ned had nearly met their fate.

"They're history," he shouted back into the building. Nancy assumed he was speaking to Hagan behind him. She gestured to Ned and counted silently, "One, two, three . . ."

They both moved together, suddenly and explosively. Nancy reached out and grabbed Garraty by the collar, yanking him out of the doorway. At the same time, Ned crashed his shoulder into the door, slamming it shut.

Garraty stumbled on his way out, and Nancy cracked him across the back of the neck with a stunning karate chop. The man dropped to his hands and knees, and she saw his gun fall out of his hand. She could hear Hagan banging against the door, trying to get out, as Ned strained to hold it shut.

"Garraty's out!" Nancy said to Ned.

Ned was leaning hard to keep the door closed, and now he said, "I think Hagan's gone—he's not banging anymore!"

"He's probably making a break for it. We've got to stop him!" Nancy called to Ned. Together they pulled the door open.

The interior of the ride was dark. "Hagan must have switched off the lights," Nancy guessed.

They slipped into the Tunnel of Love together and cautiously moved forward. They reached the door that led to the underground tunnel. It was open.

"He must have gone back down there," Nancy said. "Come on!"

Suddenly a spotlight clicked on, and the ride gyrated into operation. Nancy heard machinery moving, and the sound of a train approaching on the tracks. On a balcony to her right, the mechanical figure of a gypsy gestured eerily. Then the spotlight clicked off. A shot rang out, and a bullet whizzed past Nancy's ear. She and Ned dropped to the floor.

"It's Hagan!" Ned cried. "He's someplace back in the Tunnel of Love."

"Hagan, give up, you can't win!" Nancy called out. She knew that by now George must have called the sheriff's office. "The police know we're out here!"

Hagan's only response was the crack of another gunshot. Then the big man burst out of the darkness, charging past them as he made a break for the door that led down into the tunnels.

Nancy grabbed for Hagan. Her fingers clutched at his ankle. He tripped and stumbled through the door, screaming as he fell headfirst down the steps. There was a terrific crash, and then the sound of Hagan groaning.

Nancy and Ned raced to the top of the steps and peered down. The force of the big man's impact had been so great that the rickety stairs had collapsed. Now, he lay sprawled on the tunnel floor, the broken staircase pinning him down.

"We've got him now!" Ned cried out. "Should we go down and see how he is?"

"Let's let the police do the honors," Nancy said, her breathing still ragged.

"Fine," Ned replied, wrapping her in his arms and holding her tight against his strong chest.

Then he tilted her chin toward him. "Now, as I recall, you owe me a kiss."

"So Rand Hagan was working with Garraty all along," Adriana Polidori said, crossing her long legs in front of her. She was wearing a black silk jumpsuit with a patent leather belt. "I can hardly believe it. And he murdered my uncle—" She shook her head, an expression of deep sorrow crossing her face.

She was sitting on one of the mahogany chairs in Carson Drew's office, the morning after Garraty and Rand had been captured. George lounged in the seat next to her, with Ned perched on the arm. Carson was at his desk, and Nancy stood behind him, gazing out the window.

Nancy and Ned had spent a good part of the night before at the Conklin Falls Police Station explaining the intricacies of Garraty's plot to Sheriff Pulaski. Hagan had suffered some minor injuries from his fall, but the sheriff had assured Nancy that he would be well enough to stand trial with his partner.

Now Nancy turned to Adriana. "He also murdered Benny Gotnick," she commented.

"And did his best to kill Nancy and me," Ned added.

Carson reached out and grabbed Nancy's hand. "Needless to say, I'm overjoyed that a certain detective—with the help of her boyfriend—is responsible for putting him away."

Adriana looked at Nancy, her eyes still shining with tears. "I don't know how to thank you," she said.

"Nor I," came a deep voice at the door.

It was Mikhail Grigov. He had his shoulder against the doorframe and was watching them intently.

"I've been less than cordial to you, Nancy, I know," he went on, giving her a wry grin. "But as far as I'm concerned, you're a heroine. I'll never forget what you've done for Adriana."

Nancy bowed her head toward him, accepting the compliment gracefully.

"However, I still wish you could convince this stubborn woman to give up Riverfront Park," he said, sweeping his hand toward Adriana theatrically.

The magician laughed. "Never! Polidori's Magicworld lives!" But then she sighed. "Of course, we'll have to see what the city is going to do about cleaning up Garraty's illegal dump site. And then I'll want to explore the possibility of filling in the tunnels as well as hiring people to rebuild the whole backstage area of the auditorium."

"That'll take anywhere from six months to a year," Carson put in.

"That's right," Adriana agreed. "Which means that Riverfront Park must remain closed for this season. I shudder to think about the unsuspecting crowds who passed through the park while that poisonous waste sat in the ground beneath them."

"So what will you do now?" George asked.

Grigov spoke up. "Adriana has agreed to tour with me," he said with a smile.

Nancy glanced over at her father, but his expression remained impassive.

"I've got to work," Adriana explained. "That's the only way I'll be able to put the past behind me." She looked at Carson then. "But I'll be back next winter with a whole briefcase full of plans."

For a minute Carson caught her glance and held it.

"Freda Clarke will love that," George commented wryly, reaching down to her injured foot.

Ned punched her playfully in the arm. "Stop messing around with your cast.

"But it itches," she complained.

"Actually," Adriana began, "I got a call from Freda Clarke last night. She apologized and said that she wouldn't oppose my future plans for Riverfront Park."

"Pretty classy," Ned said.

Still, Nancy felt deeply sorry for the woman Vince Garraty had so callously manipulated. She decided to take George for a visit to Chris Clarke just as soon as she could.

They chatted on for a little while, then Adriana rose to go. Nancy and her father came around the desk and walked her to the door.

The magician paused there briefly to shake

hands with George and Ned and give Nancy a hug. She turned to Carson.

"I warn you, you haven't seen the last of me," she said wistfully.

Carson grinned. "I should hope not. You're my client, after all."

Nancy glanced toward Grigov, who'd been watching the proceedings quietly. She wondered what he thought but decided not to worry about it.

Then Adriana was gone.

George and Ned followed her out the door.

"So, Dad," Nancy said gently once they were alone, "are you sorry to see her go?"

"Yes and no," he said with a small shrug.

"She's a beautiful and fascinating woman," Nancy reminded him.

"That's true," he replied, then smiled. "But I already have one of those. And that's enough for any man!"

Nancy's next case:

Nancy has come to Yellowstone National Park at the urgent request of her boyfriend, Ned. His professor organized the trip in order to research the marmot, an animal native to the park. But the natural wonders of Yellowstone have turned into a setting for unnatural danger as the furry little mammal becomes the focus of human greed and hard crime.

Nancy arrives on the scene to discover that someone has been stealing the prized marmots and is determined to sell them on the black market. And not only are the animals at risk, but several members of the project have also been attacked. One is already in the hospital, Ned has suffered a blow to the head, and Nancy could be the next to fall into the poacher's deadly trap . . . in *An Instinct for Trouble*, Case #95 in the Nancy Drew Files™.